It was the way she'd always wanted a man to look at her...

Like he wanted to consume Kat, body and soul.

Sawyer looked almost as though he was on the verge of kissing her. A part of her wished he would.

But something had changed in the silence. It was almost electric.

"Aren't you going to say anything?" he asked.

"What do you want me to—"

That's when his lips pressed into hers. Heat spread quickly through her veins, making her aware of every feverish beat of her heart.

Kat didn't pull away from Sawyer. She couldn't have even if she wanted to. Her body leaned into him instead, craving more even though it was the last thing she needed right now.

This buttoned-up businessman was hiding a skilled lover beneath that boring exterior.

And the longer he touched her, the more she wished that it really had been Sawyer Steele in her bed that night three months ago...

* * *

From Seduction to Secrets is part of the Switched! series by Andrea Laurence.

Dear Reader,

In *From Mistake to Millions*, I decided that the Steele family had identical twin sons—Finn and Sawyer. I didn't know what they would get up to, but I knew I was planting a seed that would grow into a great story later on. When I wrapped up the synopsis for *From Riches to Redemption*, I knew the story would end with a woman crashing Morgan's wedding reception and slapping Sawyer across the face. Again, I didn't know why at the time, but I knew it needed to happen.

Sometimes that's how stories begin—with a kernel of an idea that becomes more. And that's how Kat and Sawyer came together. With a literal bang. Then, I had to figure out what he did to deserve it. It was a fun journey to find out, and I hope you enjoy reading about it.

If you enjoyed Sawyer and Kat's story, tell me by visiting my website at www.andrealaurence.com, like my fan page on Facebook (authorandrealaurence), or follow me on Twitter (@andrea_laurence), Instagram (@aclaurence) and Bookbub (andrea-laurence). I'd love to hear from you!

Enjoy,

Andrea

ANDREA LAURENCE

FROM SEDUCTION TO SECRETS

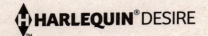

HARLEQUIN®DESIRE

Recycling programs
for this product may
not exist in your area.

ISBN-13: 978-1-335-20885-9

From Seduction to Secrets

Copyright © 2020 by Andrea Laurence

Printed in U.S.A.

HARLEQUIN®
www.Harlequin.com

Andrea Laurence is an award-winning contemporary author who has been a lover of books and writing stories since she learned to read. A dedicated West Coast girl transplanted into the Deep South, she's constantly trying to develop a taste for sweet tea and grits while caring for her boyfriend and an old bulldog. You can contact Andrea at her website: www.andrealaurence.com.

Books by Andrea Laurence

Harlequin Desire

Millionaires of Manhattan
What Lies Beneath
More Than He Expected
His Lover's Little Secret
The CEO's Unexpected Child
Little Secrets: Secretly Pregnant
Rags to Riches Baby
One Unforgettable Weekend
The Boyfriend Arrangement

Switched!

From Mistake to Millions
From Riches to Redemption
From Seduction to Secrets

Visit her Author Profile page at Harlequin.com, or andrealaurence.com, for more titles.

You can also find Andrea Laurence on Facebook, along with other Harlequin Desire authors, at www.Facebook.com/HarlequinDesireAuthors!

One

As weddings go, it was a nice enough one. Sawyer Steele hadn't been to many, but knowing his parents, it was probably an extravagant and expensive affair. Perhaps the greatest wedding ever held in Charleston. He wouldn't know the difference. It wasn't exactly Sawyer's thing. But his baby sister, Morgan, was celebrating her big day, so of course he was there to smile for pictures and eat cake. Not everyone could get shipped off to work a deal in China and miss it like Finn did.

It was probably strategy on Trevor Steele's part to have his most troublesome son out of the country for the event. Sawyer's twin was the one most likely to cause the bulk of their father's headaches. He could count on Sawyer and Tom, the oldest son, to attend and behave. As such, Sawyer had had his tuxedo dry-cleaned, his dark blond curls cut short and found a suitable date to bring with him. That was all that was really required of him tonight. Behave. Don't make a scene. Make sure Morgan is happy. Easy enough.

Now the event was starting to wind down. They'd eaten, said a million toasts, had all the requisite dances and cut into the towering ivory-and-gold confection his sister had chosen for her cake. A few more dances and they should be waving sparklers and seeing his sister and her new husband off to start their lives together. He was good with that. The bow tie he was wearing felt like it was getting tighter around his throat with each passing hour.

Glancing over, he noticed his date, Serena—a woman he'd met a few weeks earlier at a conference—eyeballing the people on the dance floor. He decided it was time to take her for a spin at last. Sawyer wasn't a dancer by any stretch, but he could manage a simple waltz for formal occasions. All the Steele children had been forced through junior cotillion to pick up some basic skills like that. They lived in the South, after all, and etiquette was paramount in the social circles he was forced into as one of the Steeles.

"Would you like to dance?" he asked Serena. The buxom blonde had chosen a low-cut, pale blue sheath dress that gave off some Cinderella vibes with her golden hair pulled up into a bun. She looked very pretty. At the same time, he just couldn't muster up much enthusiasm for her. She didn't have a very memorable personality. She actually reminded him of one of his mother's beautiful, priceless antiques. Lovely to look at, but mostly decorative.

His brother Finn preferred a sports car type girlfriend. Sexy, high performance and exciting to drive, so to speak. Those women were as high maintenance as the cars and likely to get Finn in trouble before too long.

Sawyer's ex, Mira, had been a Ferrari if ever he saw one. After that, he'd decided that maybe a roomy, luxury SUV was more his speed. Beautiful, adventurous, flexible, and if you took good care of it, it would reward your efforts for years to come.

But Serena looked so much like Mira that he instinctively wanted to call her by his ex's name, and had to stop himself each time. They looked so similar that his feelings about how things had ended with Mira may have been souring how he felt about Serena. Or maybe Serena just wasn't as much fun on the road as she appeared in the dealership.

"Sure, I'd love to dance," she said with a smile.

Oh well. There was nothing he would or could do about it tonight. He took her hand and led her to the illuminated dance floor, where at least twenty other couples were gliding along to a romantic old Sinatra song. He wrapped his arm around her waist and they started to sway slowly to the music.

It was then, with her pressed close against him, that he realized taking a woman to a wedding on a third date was way too soon. He had to bring a plus one, but it made things feel more serious than they were. They'd had drinks and dinner so far, and if this wedding hadn't come up, they might've gone to a movie. Maybe not even that, so he certainly didn't need her getting overly romantic notions when he didn't plan on a fourth date.

His gaze fell on a woman entering the ballroom. Even from this distance, she instantly captured his attention with fair skin that stood out against her black cocktail dress and bright auburn hair. She looked around the room, searching for someone. And then their eyes met. In an instant, it was like Sawyer had been hit directly in the gut. He'd never felt anything like that before. It was powerful. It made him forget all about the woman in his arms. At least for a moment.

Then he noticed the angry look on the newcomer's face and wondered if it wasn't attraction he was feeling so much as a woman's fury.

She moved quickly through the crowd toward him. Sawyer was frozen in place on the dance floor—unable to pull away from the hold the redhead had on him even though his brain was telling him to escape.

Then, at last, she arrived. "You skeevy little prick!"

The angry shout cut through the sounds in the ballroom like a knife. The dancers paused, and even the orchestra was startled into an awkward silence. Everyone turned to see the stunning redhead standing at the edge of the dance floor. Now she was only a few feet away from Sawyer, with her eyes still focused directly on him.

He'd thought for a moment that maybe he was in someone else's line of fire. He looked over his shoulder, but no one was there. Was she really talking to *him*? Shouting at him? That wasn't possible.

"Who is that woman, Sawyer?" his date asked.

That was a really good question. He'd never seen her before in his life. He certainly would've remembered a woman with hair like waves of fire and skin as flawless and pale as a porcelain doll. Even as angry as she was, he wanted to know more about her. Sawyer shook his head. "I have no idea. Can I help you, miss?"

"Can you help me?" she repeated bitterly. "Yes. You can hold still." The angry woman walked up to him and slapped him hard across the face.

He was too stunned to respond for a moment. He'd never been slapped before. Somehow, being hit by a stranger made it that much worse. She hadn't hurt him, not really. It just stung, but he could feel the emotion behind the slap. She'd wanted to hurt him, and for good reason. He just didn't know what that was.

There was a collective gasp as the whole ballroom seemed equally aghast, then a murmur as everyone started discussing what was going on. Out of the corner of his eye, Sawyer could see a couple brawny security guards his father had hired for the party making their way across the room to deal with the situation. Given that the last two events at the house had ended in a kidnapping and a bombing, respectively, it was a good move to have a little extra help in that regard.

"I'm going to have to ask you to come with us, ma'am," one of the guards, wearing a black suit and an earpiece, said.

The redhead hesitated for only a moment before she spun on her heel and marched out of the ballroom with the two guards right behind her. She'd done what she'd come here to do, apparently.

Although he knew he shouldn't abandon his date to chase down the stranger, he had to go after the woman and figure out what was going on. "I'll be right back."

Serena nodded, and he jogged out of the ballroom and into the entry hall to see if he could find where security had taken the woman. Sawyer glanced around, catching a blur of movement out of the corner of his eye as the men escorted the woman out the front door.

He chased her across the marble entry and pushed past the guards as they came back inside without her. At the top of the front stairs, he looked down and saw the woman waiting for a parking attendant to bring her car.

"I told you to keep it close!" she shouted at one of the men his parents had hired to manage all the cars at the wedding. "This wasn't going to take long. Especially with those goons seeing me out after less than a minute." She nervously glanced over her shoulder, and that was when she spied Sawyer standing at the top of the stairs.

"Do you normally wear black to weddings?" he asked. Asking why she'd slapped him seemed like jumping ahead in a conversation he wasn't ready to wrap up so quickly. "Isn't that against the rules or something?"

She sighed and crossed her hands over her chest. "It was the only nice dress I had that still fit. No offense to your sister. Anyway, don't mind me," she said. "Security has made it clear I'm not welcome, so I'm leaving. Go on back to your hot blonde. You've obviously moved on."

Sawyer took a few steps down the stairs to get closer, but out of arm's reach of the woman. He wasn't getting hit twice in one night. "I'm sorry, there's been some kind of mistake, I think. Do I know you?" The stinging welt on his cheek suggested that he did, but he was certain he'd never laid eyes on her before. She was stunning, even in the plain strapless black dress and simple makeup she was wearing. Her red hair shimmered in the moonlight, and fat curls cascaded over her bare shoulders.

No, he would remember meeting her.

"Are you serious?" She rolled her eyes, which were a dark shade of green like antique emeralds, and shook her head. "You ignored me for weeks after we got together, then when I finally track you down, you act like you have no idea what I'm even talking about. What? Are you going to tell me your evil doppelgänger slept with me, not you?"

Sawyer opened his mouth to argue, then

stopped cold. Now it all started to make sense. Why hadn't he realized this sooner? Women slapped his brother all the time. Or at least they should. It might help things. "I think you're actually looking for my twin brother, not me."

"That's an even better excuse," she said.

"It's not an excuse. Ask anyone in the party and they'll tell you I have an identical twin brother. Most people can't tell us apart."

She narrowed her gaze at him for a moment. "So you're saying you're not Sawyer Steele?"

Sawyer stopped as he opened his mouth to answer. It was one thing for her to confuse him with his brother, but this was different. "No, I *am* Sawyer Steele. But I think you're looking for my twin, Finn Steele."

The woman turned to him with her hands curled up in fists at her sides. "Are you implying that I'm some kind of slut?"

His eyes grew large with surprise. Sawyer was usually pretty good with people, very diplomatic at handling bad situations, but he couldn't say the right thing to this woman for some reason. Her hair was as fiery as her temper, it seemed. "What? No, of course not."

"You just told me I don't know the name of a man I had sex with," she said, pointing at him accusingly.

"That's not what I meant." He held out his hands in surrender and slowly came down the stairs to stand on the brick patio where she was waiting. He hoped that she would take a minute to breathe and calm down. "People get my brother and me mixed up all the time, is all. I'm telling you I've never seen you in my life, so that's the only explanation that makes sense. What is your name?"

"Katherine McIntyre." She said it with an insulted tone, as though he should know her name. "I go by Kat, if that helps jog your memory."

Sawyer frowned. To be honest, the name did sound familiar, but he was certain he'd never seen her before, much less had sex with her. He glanced down over the tightly fitting black dress, which clung to her curves and stopped just above the knee to highlight her shapely legs. He was decidedly disappointed that she'd spent the night with his brother and not him. He wasn't entirely sure that he had a type, but Kat set off all the right bells and whistles. She was a bright red Lamborghini if he'd ever seen one.

When his face didn't light up with recognition, she continued speaking. "We met at the Charleston's Best awards at the aquarium about three months ago. We had a lot of champagne, we talked, and when we got tired of looking at fish,

we got a hotel room and got…better acquainted."
Kat looked at him with a pointed expression.

Sawyer didn't remember going to an event at
the aquarium. Actually, he was certain he hadn't,
although he remembered something was being
held there a while back. That was it—he hadn't
been feeling great that day. He'd gotten a stomach
bug, but he was supposed to attend as the Steele
family representative to accept their award while
his parents were wrapped up in finalizing wedding details. He hadn't gone. In fact, he'd bribed
his twin brother to go to the event in his place.
Finn hadn't wanted to attend, either. Sawyer had
been forced to give him his new Jet Ski in ex-
change for going to the party.

Damn it to hell.

The realization of what really happened washed
over him like a wave. Sawyer brought a hand to
his face and rubbed furiously at it in frustration.
It had been years since Finn had done something
like this. Maybe even since college. Back then,
he'd liked to meet girls at bars and give them Sawyer's name instead of his own. He was never sure
if his brother just did it for a laugh, or to keep the
girls from tracking him down, but Sawyer had
earned quite a reputation on campus without doing
a single thing to get it. But now they were in their

thirties. Thirty-three, to be exact. Way too old for this kind of childish bullshit.

"I think I know what the problem is."

"The sex was so amazing you blocked it from your memory because you knew you'd never experience anything that good again?"

His jaw dropped open for a moment, then he shook his head. He'd never been so jealous of Finn in his whole life. "Uh, no. I was supposed to attend that event, but my brother went in my place. Apparently he didn't bother to tell anyone he wasn't me."

"He was wearing a name tag that said Sawyer Steele," she argued.

Sawyer wasn't surprised. "Yeah. Knowing Finn, he just went with it and pretended to be me so our father wouldn't know I bailed on the party."

Kat stopped for a moment, her mind visibly racing to process what he was telling her. "And when he kissed me? When he got a hotel room? Wouldn't that have been a good time to mention that he wasn't really you?"

"A perfect time, and I have no idea why he didn't. Listen, I'm really sorry about all this. My brother is…the trickster of the family. If he were here right now, I'd drag him outside and make him apologize for lying, but he's actually in Beijing for business. He'll be there a few weeks more, but I'll be sure to pass along your message, slap included, when he gets back."

The redhead's bravado seemed to deflate as she listened to him talk. With her anger no longer aimed at Sawyer, she seemed smaller somehow. Almost petite compared to a moment ago. "So you're saying that the man I met was actually *Finn* Steele? I can't believe, after everything that happened, that he wouldn't tell me his real name."

Sawyer could believe it. Masquerading as his brother gave Finn free license to do what he wanted without consequence. "If you don't mind me asking, was it just a one-night thing between the two of you?"

She looked at him with conflict in her eyes. "Yes. That was the plan, at least."

That was his brother's style. Love 'em and leave 'em, regardless of what name he used. "Then I doubt he would bother to correct you if you thought he was me. In the end, what would it matter? It's just a one-night stand."

Kat's expression softened for a moment as she glanced down at the ground, her eyes hidden beneath her thick auburn lashes. "It does matter, Sawyer. That's why I've crashed this party even though it's obvious he doesn't want to see me again. It matters because I'm pregnant with his child."

* * *

Katherine McIntyre had never seen a man's face blanch to a ghostly white so quickly. Even at night, with the patio light behind him, she could see the blood drain from his face and his attractive tan fade. If he hadn't seemed so steady on his feet until now, she might worry that he was about to pass out.

She wasn't sure why he was so upset about the news. He wasn't the father. He wasn't pregnant. He hadn't just found out he'd slept with a lying cheat. She was the one having a terrible night. Sure, he'd been slapped by mistake and would have a lot of explaining to do when he saw his date again, but this was hardly his problem.

The valet brought her car around at last. "I'm sorry. It took a few times for it to turn over," he said.

Kat glanced to where the valet was waiting and then back at the dumbstruck Steele heir. "I'd better go."

He reached out to her, almost appearing to surprise himself as he did it. "Wait. Come back inside and we can talk some more."

She was tempted to say yes. There was a kindness in his eyes that beckoned her to climb the steps and chat with him. It was different than what she'd seen in those familiar eyes before, so his story seemed to hold up. While identical in appearance, the Steele twins were very different men. But talking made no sense when Sawyer wasn't the one she needed to talk to. At least about the baby.

A white Rolls Royce started up the driveway and the front doors of the house opened. People started pouring out onto the stairs. It must be time for the bride and groom to make their exit. Kat wasn't going to stay around for that. Even if her old Jeep wasn't in the way.

"I can't," she said. "But Saw—I mean *Finn*—should know how to reach me when he gets back to the States. Please have him call me." She reached into her purse and pulled out a business card. She'd given Finn one before, but it had likely ended up in the trash the next morning.

Sawyer glanced over his shoulder at all the people coming toward them and his jaw flexed with what looked like irritation as he reached to take the card from her hand. He sighed and nodded as he glanced down at it. "I'll make sure he calls you *before* he gets back. I'm actually going to phone and wake him up right now. He deserves it."

Kat nodded and walked around her Jeep to get inside. She told herself not to look in the rearview mirror as she pulled away, but she did it anyway. She watched Sawyer Steele as his gaze followed her into the distance. He was still watching as she turned out of the driveway and the big house disappeared from sight.

With a groan, she wrapped her fingers tightly around the steering wheel and pressed down the gas pedal. This was not how she had envisioned this night playing out. She'd just wanted to pin Sawyer—*Finn*—down to talk, the same as that first night. Pregnancy was not what she had been going for back then. Far from it. But now that it was done, she wanted to do the right thing and tell the father. If he wasn't going to return her calls, she had to find another way to reach him.

The idea was to locate him, pull him aside to talk, and take things from there. Slapping the father of her child hadn't been a part of her plan, but when she saw him dancing with that beautiful blonde, she couldn't help it. Between morning sickness and pure exhaustion, she'd been uncomfortable for the last few weeks. He could be uncomfortable for a moment or two himself.

Then she'd found out she'd hit the wrong guy and everything just unraveled. China. Her baby's father was in China and that was the least of her troubles. Her baby's father was also a "trickster" in his own brother's words, one who had no problem seducing a woman using his brother's name. That was not the kind of man she wanted in her child's life, but it was too late now. It was done and she would have to find a way to deal with the aftermath.

Kat slowly pulled into her narrow driveway and turned off the Jeep's engine. She looked over at the historic Charleston-style house she called home. Located in the heart of the Peninsula, it had always been enough for her. The twelve-hundred-square-foot structure was the perfect space for a free-spirited artist. It had plenty of light, the traditional piazza patio allowed her to work outside sometimes and, best of all…the place was paid for.

She climbed from her Jeep and went inside. Her little abode was no Steele mansion, but what was? To be honest, she really hadn't understood what kind of family she'd gotten involved with until she pulled into that driveway and got her first view of the house. The Corinthian columns, the white-washed stone, the lane of old live oak trees dripping Spanish moss on the long drive to the house…it was like something out of a Southern gothic novel. In this day and age it was the kind of place that was usually a museum, or rented out for weddings and events. But no, the Steeles actually lived there.

Kat wasn't a stranger to money. Both her parents had been successful, her father a famous mystery writer and her mother a celebrated painter. They'd done well for themselves, and when they were both killed in a car accident, their estates and life insurance policies had supported Kat through art school and allowed her to be an artist herself without worrying about starving or working a day job. Yes, she needed a new car. And yes, the house probably needed a new coat of paint, but she didn't want for much.

She tossed her purse onto the couch beside a box of woodworking tools and wood scraps. It would go with her Monday morning when she went down to the District to work. The old warehouse-turned-artist-community was where she spent most of her days. She rented a studio in the building even though she had room at the house to work. Woodworking was messy, but being there was more about community and exposure than anything else. If she wasn't working there or selling pieces to folks strolling by, she was hanging out with the other artists, who had become her family since her parents died.

Honestly, losing that place would be like losing her parents all over again. And that was what she was facing. That was why she'd gotten all dressed up and gone downtown to that stupid awards ceremony the night she'd met Finn. Because she was going to lose it all to the wheels of progress and commerce.

Four months ago, the owner of the District passed away and his children sold the building to a developer. The place would be gutted and reno- vated. It would remain an artist community—at least that's what the letters they all received said— but it would be more about selling than creating, by necessity. The rent would be tripling to cover the costs of the renovations and bring the place more in line with the new owner's vision.

Kat had the money to pay the rent at the new building, but most artists weren't so lucky. When the District reopened as a fancy, funky downtown venue for people to shop and be seen, most of the people she knew and loved would be long gone.

Walking up the stairs to her bedroom, she un- zipped her dress and let it slip to the floor on the landing. Kat stepped out of it and turned sideways to admire her slightly rounding tummy in the hall- way mirror. She'd just started to show in the last week or so. Her normally flat belly had begun to curve out, making her favorite jeans uncomfort- ably tight at the waistband. She'd told Sawyer the truth when she said this was the only dress she had that fit. Most formals weren't made of particularly forgiving fabrics.

Life didn't always turn out the way she expected it to. This baby was evidence enough of that. Kat had gone to that award ceremony to try and talk some sense into the District's new owner, Sawyer Steele. Instead, she was having his brother's baby.

Two

"You're a real piece of work, you know that?"

"What?"

As always, Finn's voice didn't betray even the slightest bit of guilt for what he might have done. There was only an edge of sleepiness, which was to be expected given the hour in China. At least where Finn was concerned. The average Beijing citizen was likely preparing to eat lunch by now, but his brother had still been asleep after a late Saturday night of high jinks that probably involved beautiful Chinese women and too much *baiju* to drink.

"Sawyer, you know I'm half asleep and half hungover. Why don't you just tell me what you think I've done wrong instead of making me guess. Then we can move straight on to you yelling, and I can take some ibuprofen and go back to sleep."

"You're not going back to sleep, Finn. And I don't *think* I know what you did, I'm certain of it. And it's a big one this time."

"I doubt that. You're prone to overreaction, like Father."

Sawyer swallowed an insult. He wasn't going to let his brother bait him. Finn knew how much he hated being compared to their father. Yes, they shared an affinity for keeping the peace and avoiding drama, but that was about it. "You know, when I gave you that Jet Ski for going in my place to the Charleston's Best awards, it was because I wanted the night to go smoothly."

"As I recall it did go smoothly," Finn replied. "I picked up a nice plaque for the company awards case, Dad didn't figure out you skipped, and I got a new Jet Ski. Win-win."

"Yes, well, that was because everyone at the party thought you were me. I thought we were past the childish identical-twin games, Finn."

There was a moment of silence on the line, but Sawyer knew it wasn't out of guilt. Knowing Finn, he was trying to figure out how to weasel out of getting into trouble.

"Okay, who told on me? There's no way you could know that I let everyone think I was you," he said at last. "It's been months since that party and there hasn't been a peep about it since then."

"Well, that's not entirely true. Apparently the redhead you seduced that night while you were pretending to be me has been trying to get in touch with you. Me. *Us*."

Finn groaned and audibly flopped back against the pillows. "The redhead. Yeah. That was a hell of a night, but I wasn't really interested in seeing her again. She's gorgeous, don't get me wrong, but she's not my usual type. She's too artsy and academic. She's more your type, I think."

That was true enough, but Sawyer wasn't interested in walking into the hot mess his brother had left behind. "Well, to be honest, I don't think she was wanting to see you again, either, but she doesn't have a choice."

Finn chuckled. "And why is that? She can't get enough of me? She wouldn't be the first."

"No, because she's having your baby, you thoughtless idiot. How could you not take precautions for a one-night stand? You know better than that."

"Whoa, whoa, whoa," Finn said, suddenly sounding very awake on the other end of the call. "My baby? The redhead is pregnant? Well, it can't be mine."

"Her name is Kat," Sawyer corrected with an irritated tone. For some reason it grated on him that Finn was starting a family with a woman whose name he couldn't remember. "And she says it's yours. Actually, she thought it was mine until I figured out what you did and got her straightened out."

"No, it's not my baby," Finn insisted. "Listen, you may think I'm stupid, but that is one area where I don't take chances. In all these years, I've never even had a scare. Nothing was different about my night with her. She's mistaken. It's someone else's baby."

Sawyer would've liked to believe that his brother took anything seriously, especially something like this. But he'd seen the pained look in those big green eyes. She believed her story, and he wanted to believe her. But belief and trust were two different things. "Are you sure? There were no rips, no slipups?"

"No, I'm telling you, I know how to use one properly."

"Fine." There had to be another explanation for why it failed. "Did you bring the condoms or did she?"

There was a pause as Finn lay in bed, likely sorting through his romantic memory bank. "Usually I do, but I remember I didn't have any on me that night. It was supposed to be a boring party, which is why I pretended to be you, to spice things up. She had the condoms."

That made Sawyer's stomach ache with worry. If Finn wasn't in control of them at all times, anything could happen. "That means she could've sabotaged them if she wanted to. Maybe poked holes in one."

"You think she got pregnant on purpose?"

Sawyer sighed and sat back in the leather wing-back chair of the family library. He didn't know. Their father had raised them to be suspicious of women's motives. Getting pregnant was an easy way to weasel into the family, and more importantly, into their fortune. "I don't know. You know her better than I do."

"Hardly," Finn scoffed. "We flirted and looked at fish in the aquarium. I don't really know anything about…"

"Kat," Sawyer repeated. "Please remember the name of the woman who's carrying your child."

"*Might* be carrying my child," Finn corrected. "I'm not as convinced as you are."

"Yeah, well, until we know otherwise, you need to handle this situation as though it were true."

"Handle it how, Sawyer? I'm in Beijing. I couldn't even come back for Morgan's wedding. I can't just fly home in the middle of constructing the new manufacturing plant and deal with... *Kat.* Dad placed a lot of trust in me when he gave me this project. I can't screw it up or I won't get a second chance."

"And if Dad finds out that you've knocked up some stranger and walked away from the situation, it will be even worse."

Finn groaned aloud. "Please don't tell him until I have some time to think on this."

"You'd better think fast. He'll find out soon. She made quite a scene at the wedding tonight. Everyone will want to know what it was about."

"A scene?"

"Yeah." Sawyer's cheek still stung from the slap Kat had given him. "When you get back to Charleston, I'll pass her message along." He intended to hit his brother harder than Kat ever could.

"Does anyone else know?" Finn asked.

"No. I thought I'd tell you first, since she's been unsuccessful in telling you personally."

"Okay, good. Can we keep it that way for a while until I can figure out what I'm going to do?"

"I'll hold out as long as I can, but I'm not going to lie for you, Finn."

"That's fair enough. I'll give my attorney a call and see what he recommends, then take it from there. Knowing him, he'll tell me to make a big opening offer, something she can't refuse, then she'll be happy and hopefully things won't escalate. I'll keep you posted."

"Fine. But one last thing before you go, Finn."

"What's that?"

Sawyer considered his words before he said them, speaking with slow, deliberate intention. "If you ever, *ever* pretend to be me again, I'm going to mess up your face so badly no one will be able to confuse us. Am I clear?"

There was a long silence before Finn answered. "Crystal."

The line disconnected and Sawyer slipped his phone into his coat pocket. By the time he stepped out of the library and into the grand foyer, he was surprised to find that the wedding appeared to be over. Once the happy couple left, things must have wrapped up. The guests were gone, the orchestra was breaking down and the caterers were bussing the tables. He glanced around for a blonde in a pale blue gown, but Serena was nowhere to be found.

Looking at his watch, he winced when he realized how late it was. So much for telling Serena he'd be right back. She'd probably given up on him long ago. And for good. For all she knew, he'd abandoned her on the dance floor and run off with some redhead. Serena deserved someone who couldn't get thoughts of her out of his mind.

Kind of like the feisty and mysterious Kat was on Sawyer's mind right now.

He strolled into the abandoned ballroom, heading toward the wedding cake, or what was left of it. A few pieces were still sitting on china plates, waiting to be eaten, even as the caterers worked to disassemble and pack up the remaining tiers. He picked up a slice and carried it with him into the kitchen. After brewing a cup of coffee and slowly savoring his prize, he remembered the business card he'd thoughtlessly tucked into his breast coat pocket.

When he fished it out and looked down at it at last, a piece of the fluffy white cake caught in his throat. Sawyer coughed for a moment, fighting to breathe again. Then he picked up the card and reread the words that had surprised him so much the first time.

Katherine McIntyre, Artist.
The District, Floor 2, Studio 210

Suddenly he remembered why her name had sounded familiar. He hadn't lied when he said they hadn't met. He'd never laid eyes on her before. But she had emailed him, written him and called his office so many times in the last four months that his assistant had asked for a raise.

Kat was the voice of the District's resistance group. They were not happy about his plans for the building he'd purchased, and no amount of talking was budging either side of the argument. So far.

It was then that Sawyer was absolutely certain Kat's appearance at that party three months ago, and possibly in his brother's bed, was no coincidence.

Kat frowned at the misshaped hunk of wood in front of her. This was not her best work. Far from it. Honestly, it was crap. All she'd managed to produce was crap since the day she'd taken that pregnancy test and got a positive result. The creative zone had eluded her ever since then. She understood now why her parents had each been so protective of their work time and space. It was a fragile ecosystem, susceptible to imbalance when a sticky-fingered child was introduced to the situation.

That didn't bode well for her future work, but she refused to worry about it now. She would figure it out. And not the way her parents had. Locked office doors and nannies were effective, but not particularly warm and loving for a child who wanted nothing more than her family's love.

"So…" A familiar voice sounded from the entryway of her studio. "How'd last night go?"

Setting down her chisel, Kat turned to find one of her fellow artists and friends standing there in old overalls, fireproof gloves and a welding helmet. Hilda Levy rented the studio across from Kat, and despite the constant sounds of metal banging and sparks flying, she couldn't ask for a better friend to work nearby. That said, she also kept a fire extinguisher on hand in case her wood shavings and Hilda's blazing hot sparks collided.

"It went terribly," Kat confessed.

Hilda pushed her helmet up, exposing the laugh lines and quirky black cat-eye glasses she was known for. "Well, shit. What happened?"

Kat plopped down onto an old futon she kept in the corner of her studio, and Hilda followed suit. "Well, for one thing, I had the wrong guy."

Few things seemed to faze Hilda, but this caused her brow to knit in confusion. "What's that, now?"

"I didn't have sex with Sawyer Steele."

The older woman looked over the top of her glasses at Kat. "Then who the hell was it?"

"His twin brother, Finn. He just let me think he was Sawyer, for kicks or something."

"The plot thickens," Hilda said, as she leaned in with interest. "So did you talk to Finn?"

"Uh, no. After crashing the wedding and slapping Sawyer, I hightailed it out of there, after I found out the truth. I was so embarrassed by the whole thing, I wouldn't stay a moment longer. But I did find out that Finn is half a world away at the moment. So that complicates matters."

"Does it? I know I'm old, but I have heard tell of this fancy internet thing that lets people communicate around the world."

Kat rolled her eyes at her friend's deadpan commentary. "You're not old. And I'll talk to him. Eventually. Right now I'm still trying to wrap my head around the whole thing. I mean, I slept with the wrong guy. The whole reason I went to that stupid award ceremony was to talk to Sawyer. To try and convince him that his plans for the District would be detrimental to the whole art community."

"Not sleep with him," Hilda added.

"No, not sleep with him," Kat agreed. "That was…accidental. I went down in person to put him on the spot, because he wasn't returning any of my calls and I couldn't get past his stupid secretary. And it got us nowhere in the end, because not only did we never discuss his plans for the District that night, the man I met wasn't even the one who bought it."

"You didn't bring it up that night?"

Kat thought back to the dark aquarium, the

blue tank lights and the dimpled smile that had lulled her into doing something stupid. "I tried. But whenever I did, he'd change the subject. Probably so I wouldn't figure out he wasn't Sawyer and had no idea what I was talking about." She groaned and dropped her face into her hand. "I'm such an idiot."

"You're not an idiot. You were swept away by a charming billionaire after drinking too much champagne. That's no crime. Personally, I'd love to make a mistake like that. It's been a long time."

Kat couldn't help smiling at her friend. Hilda always had an outlook on life that could pull her out of the dumps when she was wallowing there. She honestly wasn't sure how she would've gotten on after her parents died without Hilda. Without everyone here at the District, actually. Hilda was like her surrogate mother now. Except she gave advice like a girlfriend, not a mom. Since Hilda had never married or had kids of her own, maternal advice wasn't her strong suit. Or so she said.

"We need to get you some," Kat said. She was a little relieved to shift the topic off herself, even for a short time.

"Oh, Lordy," Hilda exclaimed. "That shop has been closed down for so long it would take more than a good dusting to get it up and operational again."

"I'm pretty sure it all still works. There's someone out there for you. And when you meet him, you won't be able to dust off that equipment fast enough."

"I'm not so sure," Hilda replied. This time when she spoke the smile in her eyes dimmed slightly. She was lonely. Kat knew it. Her smile and attitude tried to hide the fact, but Kat knew better.

"I've seen Zeke watching you work with more than a little appreciation in his gaze."

Hilda rolled her eyes and shook her head. "Zeke? You've got to be kidding me. He just likes my work."

"Are you sure?" Kat wagged her eyebrows suggestively. The older man was a sculptor with a studio on the other side of their floor. With Kat and Hilda at the back of the building, opposite the stairs and the restrooms, there was no reason for Zeke to be over on their side. But for some reason, he always seemed to be hanging around Hilda's studio. It couldn't be just because of her metalwork.

"No," she argued. "But even if there was more to it, I'm not interested."

"Why?" Kat challenged. Hilda had spent more than a few working hours over by Zeke's studio herself.

"Because he's a widower. His wife has been

gone for a year now. Men his age don't date for love. They date because they can't function without a woman to cook and clean for them. I've avoided being someone's maid for fifty-eight years and I have no interest in starting now."

"You don't know what he wants until you ask."

Hilda sputtered for a moment before turning to Kat with a disgruntled expression on her face. "Why are we talking about my love life? You're the one in the midst of a crisis."

"Thanks for the reminder." Kat pushed herself up from the couch and walked over to the table, where she'd left a bottle of water earlier. She took a sip and shook her head. "His brother said he'd get in touch with Finn, and hopefully, I'll hear something soon."

"And when you do hear from him, what exactly are you going to say? Have you decided what you want to do about the whole situation yet?"

Kat frowned. "Yes and no. My baby is my baby, end of story there. But as far as Finn and his role in our lives... I don't know. I just... My whole life I've had this vision of my future and my family. It includes marriage. It always has."

"From what you've said so far, this Finn guy doesn't really sound like marriage material."

"He's not. Absolutely not. But the more I think about it, the more I've come to realize that it doesn't change how I want things to be. I refuse to have my child born a bastard like I was. Regardless of the circumstances."

"Your parents were together for twenty-five years," Hilda argued.

"And never married," Kat added. For whatever reason, they'd never felt it was important to do so. She got the feeling they'd actually avoided it deliberately because of the stickiness of comingling their artistic property and intellectual rights. It was such a silly reason in her eyes.

"So what? It's not the 1950s anymore. Most of those *Karwashians* aren't married and they're having kids left and right."

"It's Kardashian," Kat corrected, wishing she didn't know enough about them to notice Hilda mangling their name. "And some of them are married. But it's not the point."

"Then tell me what is the point, honey."

"I want my child to have a family."

"You hardly know this guy."

"Maybe it's better I don't. Maybe we should just jump in with both feet and see what happens. It's possible we only stay married a year. Or we barely make it past the baby's birthday before we call it quits. I can't tell you how it will end up. But I can't help but think it's the right thing to do for my baby."

"I'm not sure the Steele family is going to be as receptive as you're wanting them to be. They have more money than the state of South Carolina. Even if Finn agrees to marry you, there's going to be lawyers involved at every step. Prenuptial agreements. Custody arrangements. It's not going to be the least bit romantic."

"I don't care about romance and I don't care about the money. I have enough of that. I only want my baby to have what's his or hers. I don't need anything other than a father for my child. I want better for my baby than I had."

"Okay." Hilda gave a heavy sigh. "If you're determined, then I wish you the best of luck marrying into that family. As for me," she said, pushing up from the low futon with a groan, "I've got to get some work done. The clock is ticking on our time here and it's going to be a nightmare hauling all my scrap metal away."

Kat looked around her own studio, feeling guilty that she could afford to stay when others couldn't. She'd still have to pack up and move out for a few months while they renovated, but she could come back. "You're not moving out for good, Hilda. I promise. No matter what happened between Finn and myself, I still intend to pin down that jerk Sawyer Steele, and get him to change his mind about the District. Of course, now he probably thinks I'm just some gold-digging slut and won't take me seriously."

Hilda's gaze shifted over Kat's shoulder as her eyes widened behind her thick black glasses. She bit at her lip and gently shook her head.

Kat realized she was standing with her back to the entrance of her studio. "He's right behind me, isn't he?"

Hilda nodded and Kat groaned aloud.

"I might be a jerk, but if it's any consolation," a man's voice said from over her shoulder, "I don't think you're just a gold-digging slut."

Three

Kat turned slowly to look at him and he couldn't wipe the smug grin from his face. Sawyer's timing couldn't have been better if he'd tried. He'd caught her in the middle of a tirade about him, and that was fine, because he had a few choice words for her, too.

Most of those words dissipated from his mind when she was facing him. He thought she had looked beautiful at the wedding, but it didn't hold a candle to how she looked today. Her copper hair was twisted into a messy bun, with two pencils holding it in place and sawdust, like glitter, sprinkled over the top. Her face was devoid of makeup, unless you could count the smear of white paint on her cheek and a splatter of yellow paint dots across her forehead. She was wearing a tank top and a pair of denim cutoff shorts that fell at the perfect length to highlight her firm, smooth thighs.

He expected her to say something, but she stood motionless, obviously in shock at his timely appearance. Before he could say anything else, the older woman standing nearby opted to excuse herself.

"I'll let you two talk. I've got a piece to finish and five years of crap to pack up." She looked pointedly at Sawyer as she went by.

He was used to that by now. He was the big, bad real estate developer out to destroy all they held dear. At least, that was what most of the voice mail and phone messages seemed to say. Sawyer wished he could convince them that he was trying to help, but they would never see it from his point of view. They either didn't know or didn't care that the building was crumbling around them. The electrical was old and not up to code. The plumbing was putting out rust-colored water and the pressure was almost useless. The freight elevator barely passed inspection. Before long, the District was going to be condemned and they would all lose their precious studio community.

Sawyer intended to fix things. Making those fixes required a few big concessions on the tenants' parts: one, that they move out temporarily for the work to be done, and two, that their rent increase to cover the costs. When it was all said and done, he wasn't renovating this place out of the goodness of his heart. He was a businessman. He saw the potential of the District. With some improvements, it could be not only a studio community, but a place where people wanted to come. Customers. Those people would spend money.

It was a win-win in his eyes. He wished he wasn't the only one who saw that his plan was necessary to save the institution as a whole. Yes, some people might not be able to afford the rent at the new location, even with increased sales. But he'd learned a long time ago that he couldn't make everyone happy, so he'd stopped trying.

He watched the older woman leave, then turned back to where Kat was standing, red-faced, in front of him. "You know, when we first met, your name sounded familiar, but I didn't connect the dots. It wasn't until I looked at your business card." He fished it from his pocket and held it up. "Then all the pieces came together."

"What are you doing here, Sawyer?" She wiped self-consciously at her face, but the paint stayed stubbornly in place. "Have your lawyers put together some payoff package to make me go away?"

Sawyer smiled and turned toward the collection of works in progress she had scattered around her studio space. "I'm not sure what the lawyers have in mind. Or if anyone has told them yet. I told Finn he had to deal with all that." He stuffed his hands into his pockets and strolled over to admire an intricate carving of an owl on a nearby table. It was the size of a large watermelon, with big, lifelike eyes and feathers etched so delicately it seemed he could reach out and they would feel real. She was a very talented artist.

"So you've told Finn?"

He pulled away from the owl and turned to see Kat biting anxiously at her lower lip. He wanted to run his thumb across that same lip to protect it from her abuses. Instead, he kept his hands deep in his trouser pockets where they belonged. "The minute you left. I couldn't wake him up fast enough with the good news."

"He hasn't reached out to me."

Sawyer wasn't surprised. "I wouldn't let that worry you. I'm sure he wants to get his ducks in a row before he calls. And he has very unruly ducks. They're basically squirrels on a sugar high. It may take some time."

"I'm kinda on a set time line here," Kat said,

with one hand protectively covering the slight curve of her belly. "I hope he doesn't take too long, because like it or not, his baby is going to be here come winter."

"I'm sure he'll be in touch. Once the shock wears off. He really wasn't expecting to hear from you again."

"Well, considering he didn't give me the right name, I'm not surprised."

"Yes. I think that's the last time he'll play that game, though. He's far too fond of his good looks to risk them by pretending to be me again. I do have to wonder, though."

"Wonder what?"

Sawyer turned and looked at Kat, who was standing a few feet away. He could easily imagine her in some slinky dress, all dolled up to go to the party and hunt down Sawyer Steele. She intended to get her way, no matter what it took. "It made me wonder how the night would've ended if it had been me there and not Finn."

To be honest, the thought had haunted him the last few days. She had come to the party to see him. To talk to him. Perhaps to seduce him. And somehow the spoils went to Finn instead. Just like usual.

"I'm sure it would've ended very differently," Kat said.

"Would it?" he asked with an arched eyebrow.

"I think so. For one thing, you probably wouldn't have dodged my questions about the District and we could've had a real dialogue about it. And for another, you don't have Finn's…*charisma*."

"Is that what you call it?" Sawyer chuckled. "I typically describe that skill set a little differently. I'm sure that played right into your hands, though."

Kat narrowed her gaze at him, her nose wrinkling in thought and a line creasing between her auburn eyebrows. "What's that supposed to mean?"

"I mean, if you went to that party with the intention of doing whatever it took to get your way… Finn made it easier. I would've been a more difficult mark."

"Wait a minute," Kat said, her hands held out defensively. "Are you suggesting that I deliberately went to the party to seduce you? As though I could be so good in bed that you would just change your mind about the District renovations and do whatever I asked?"

Sawyer shrugged. "I don't know what you were thinking. It does seem pretty convenient, though, the more I think about it. Nothing you were doing was yielding any results. If angry calls and letters didn't work, sympathetic news articles didn't work, protests didn't work…why not try a little honey instead of vinegar?"

"I did not go to that party with the intention of giving you any...*honey*! I went to that event to talk to you, because you wouldn't return any of my calls. It was the only way I could think of to pin you on the spot and make you listen to my side of the situation."

"And yet somehow you ended up sleeping with the man who claimed to be me. Sounds like you're quite the overachiever."

The steam was practically coming out of Kat's ears, and he found he quite liked her when she was angry. The flushed cheeks, the bright eyes, pursed lips...he imagined it wouldn't be much different from how she'd look in the throes of passion. He could just envision her auburn hair across the pillowcase, her sharp nails digging into the flesh of his back...

"Of all the arrogant, insulting things you could say!" Kat sputtered for a moment, at a loss for words before she shook her head. "I was a damned fool to go down there that night. A fool to think that you could be reasoned with. All you rich people care about is your bottom line. The people here are just walking, talking rent payments to you. You don't give a damn about what this place means to the tenants here. You don't care about the community that's grown here over the years, or how you're going to destroy it to make a buck!"

Her anger suddenly wasn't so attractive anymore and she was starting to rub Sawyer the wrong way. She wanted to know why he was doing what he was doing? Well, he was going to tell her. He closed the gap between them and spoke with cold, quiet anger, mere inches from her face. "And you don't seem to care that the rent I'm currently collecting barely covers the utilities for this place. There certainly isn't enough left over to do any repairs and it's falling down around you."

Sawyer pointed to the peeling plaster overhead. "That's going to come crashing down on you sooner or later. The sewer lines are going to fail and flood the ground floor. That wood lathe of yours could overtax the electrical circuits at any moment and set the building on fire. Who is going to fix that? Who is going to pay for all that? The previous owner just ignored the place and cashed the checks. Sure, rent was cheap, but there's a cost, and the building has paid the price for all of you. It's your turn to pay up, and no amount of sweet-talking or seduction is going to change that."

Kat was at a loss for words. It didn't happen very often, but Sawyer seemed to be able to render her mute. Especially when he stood this close to her. Yes, his words were icy cold with restrained anger and frustration, but she could feel the heat radiating off his body. His words were just static noise in the background, with her pounding heart drowning out everything but its sensual rhythm. She knew she should take a step back, reclaim her personal space and counter his argument with more pointed words, but she couldn't make herself do it. Her body wanted to move nearer and close the gap between them.

It was ridiculous. Foolish. But she couldn't help but be confused whenever she was around Sawyer. She was haunted by memories of a night in a downtown hotel room…memories of a man who looked like Sawyer. A man she'd thought *was* Sawyer. Somehow it felt like the most natural thing in the world to reach out and touch him like she had before. Her libido couldn't tell the difference between the two identical men.

But her brain knew. And it knew that was all a lie. Those memories, that man… It wasn't Sawyer she remembered. And no matter how familiar those dark eyes or that dimpled smile, it wasn't the same person. This man was a stranger. A stranger who intended to take away everything she held dear to make a buck. Sure, he wanted to make necessary improvements, but the fancy, downtown art scene he had in mind was a far cry from what the tenants truly needed. The necessary repairs weren't the changes driving the rent out of the realm of possibility for most of the artists. It was the coffee shop, the concert venue, the paved parking lot and the high-end landscaping with dancing fountains.

It was a great response, exactly what she wanted to say, but the argument eluded her when Sawyer gazed at her this way. It wasn't how Finn had looked at her. And yet it was the way she'd always wanted a man to look at her. Like he wanted to consume her, body and soul.

Even in his anger, Sawyer seemed almost as though he was on the verge of kissing her. A part of her wished he would, even if just to end this fight.

Okay, not *just* to end the fight.

Kat's gaze met Sawyer's. In the quiet stillness between them, they seemed to be even closer now. She could feel his breath softly brushing over her skin. Something had changed in the silence and it seemed that he noticed it, as well. It was almost an electricity.

"Aren't you going to say anything?" he asked.

"What do you want me to—"

That's when his lips pressed into hers and a warm tingle shot down her spine. His heat spread quickly through her veins, making her aware of every feverish beat of her heart. Kat didn't pull away from Sawyer. She couldn't even if she wanted to. Her body leaned into him instead, craving more even though it was the last thing she needed right now.

His arms slipped around her waist and pulled her tight against the hard wall of his body. It was then, with every inch of her curves molded against his hard angles, that Kat knew for certain appearances were deceiving. For one thing, Sawyer might look like Finn, but he certainly didn't kiss like him. His twin might have the reputation of being a playboy, but Sawyer had obviously gone for quality over quantity where women were concerned. As he deepened the kiss, his tongue slid leisurely along her bottom lip as though he had all the time in the world to study every inch of her. It elicited a groan of pleasure deep in Kat's throat—a sound she didn't even know she could make until that moment.

This buttoned-up businessman was hiding a skilled lover beneath that boring exterior. And the longer he touched her, the more she wished that it really had been Sawyer Steele in her bed that night three months ago.

But it wasn't.

The thought that was like a lightning bolt of reality. What the hell was she doing? Kissing Sawyer Steele when she wanted to marry his brother?

It took every ounce of determination she had, but she pulled away from his embrace and stepped back out of Sawyer's sphere of influence. Once she got some distance between them again, it was easier to control her impulses and regain what little composure she had left.

This was the wrong Steele twin. They looked alike, but they acted very differently, and like it or not, Sawyer was not the one she needed in her life. Finn was her baby's father. Kissing his brother did nothing but muddy the waters and make an already complicated situation even more so.

Kat covered her lips with her hand, hoping she could somehow wipe away the tingle that lingered there from Sawyer's kiss. It didn't work.

"Did I do something wrong?" Sawyer asked, seeming almost startled by her sudden retreat.

No. Somehow he'd done everything right. Yes, Finn was charming, but Sawyer had different powers that Kat couldn't resist. "No, you didn't. I just… I think that was probably a mistake."

She watched Sawyer's jaw flex and tighten as if he was holding something in. She wished he would just say it, but he didn't seem like that kind of man. He knew when to use restraint, unlike his twin, who did or said whatever he wanted whenever he liked.

His gaze followed her hand as it dropped protectively to her belly on reflex. Then his eyes squeezed shut for a moment and he nodded. "You're right. I overstepped."

"You didn't. We both——"

"No." He held up his palm to halt any further argument from her. "It's my fault. You're having my brother's child. There's no excuse for my behavior."

"And *my* behavior is okay?" she asked. It had been only a moment since they kissed, and her memory still served her pretty well. Whether or not she should've been an active and enthusiastic participant, she was.

"It's not your fault. You were attracted to my brother, obviously. I look exactly like him. I can imagine it's confusing. It's an easy mistake for you to make in the moment, feeling like you're attracted to me when you're not." Sawyer stuffed his hands in his pockets and took a step backward.

"I'm not so blinded by desire as to not know who I was kissing. You two don't look exactly alike," Kat argued.

Sawyer hesitated a moment and shook his head. "We're identical twins."

Kat shook her head in turn. "Maybe genetically, but there are subtle differences. You're mirror images of each other. Your dimple is on the opposite cheek from Finn's. And your eyes…" Her voice drifted off. "There's something there that I didn't see in him."

She wasn't sure what it was yet. He was the more serious, responsible brother, but that wasn't it. Beneath all that there was a kindness in Sawyer's eyes. A softness when he looked at her that faded when he looked at anyone else. Finn's eyes had reflected only desire. At the time, that had been enough. Now that she was hoping for a future and a family with Finn, she wished she would see more when she looked in his eyes.

More like she saw in Sawyer.

That was a dangerous thought. There was no way to go back in time and choose a different brother. No way to go back and stop this whole pregnancy from happening to begin with. She had made her bed, as her mother used to say. Now she had to lie in it. With Finn.

"I'd better go," Sawyer said, as though he'd heard the thoughts in her head.

Before Kat could say another word, Sawyer Steele turned on his heel and vanished from her shop, leaving her more confused than she'd been when he arrived.

Well, that hadn't gone the way he'd intended. It had started out well enough, but kissing Kat was one of the dumbest things he'd ever done. This woman was his nemesis at the District. She was having his brother's baby through potentially nefarious means. She couldn't be trusted.

And yet, he'd done it anyway.

Sawyer walked quickly out of the building, trying to ignore the disgusted looks from the tenants as he went by. They knew exactly who he was with his expensive suit and his dark sunglasses. He was the one who was ruining everything.

As he stepped outside into the summer sun, he could finally breathe again. As hot as it was in the parking lot, the old building was stifling without air conditioning and only a few old windows for a cross breeze. He didn't know how anyone could work here in the summer. That was number one on his list of things to fix, and if he was a tenant here, he'd be happy to pay more not to sweat to death.

As he climbed into his Audi, his cell phone rang and his brother's number came up on the screen. "Finn," he said as he answered.

"Twin," Finn responded. "How are things going at home?"

"Hmm...let's see... Our parents are badgering me relentlessly about the mystery woman at the wedding. Grandma Ingrid is home from Europe for good. Oh, and it turns out the mother of your child is the one trying to shut down my District renovations."

"Really? That must've been why she kept asking me about it that night. I dodged the questions because I didn't know the answers."

It would've been nice if his brother had bothered

to mention the inquisitive woman from the party three months ago. "Yes, apparently she came there looking for me to talk about changing my plans. Sleeping with you was just a…"

"Bonus?" Finn suggested.

"I was going to say *mistake*, but use whatever word you like."

"I've been talking to my lawyers. They recommend coming in with a high offer to keep things quiet, so they're working on a package now."

Sawyer was surprised his brother was moving so quickly with his attorneys. He'd asked his future brother-in-law, Harley Dalton, to run a background check on her, but the report wasn't back yet. "This seems awfully premature. Are you sure you want to do that before you know if the baby is yours?"

"Well, actually, that's why I'm calling. I could use your help. They can do a prenatal paternity test with a blood sample from the mother and the father. But to speed things along, it would help if you could pop by the lab and do that for me."

Sawyer shook his head in the empty cab of his SUV. "Are you serious?"

"Come on, for a standard paternity test, we share all the same markers as identical twins. It's not a murder case, it's a baby, so unless you've slept with her, too, your DNA would be enough to determine if I'm the father. Doing the testing in China and trying to send the sample to the States would be a hassle and would take forever. This can't wait until I get back either."

"Finn…"

"Please. I've got an appointment all set up if you can swing by. I'll text you the lab address. Just donate some blood and I'll handle the rest. I just need to know for certain before I tell Mom and Dad."

Somehow Sawyer doubted that Finn would be handling much of anything. "When is the appointment?"

"This afternoon at three."

Sawyer glanced at the console of his car. It was almost two, so Finn expected him to drop everything for him, per usual. "You have no idea how much you owe me for this, Finn."

"If it's a boy, we'll name him after you," Finn offered brightly.

In irritation, Sawyer hit the button to hang up the phone. "You're welcome," he snapped as he drove the car out of the District parking lot and headed for the lab.

Four

Kat came home to find a FedEx package on her doorstep. She hadn't ordered anything, so when she picked up the envelope, she eyed the return address with curiosity.

Carson, Turner and Leeds. Attorneys at Law.

Lovely. She'd been expecting this package since someone from the lawyer's office called and asked her to take a paternity test. She'd complied but thought perhaps she might actually *speak* to Finn before she received anything else from them. Guess not.

With a sigh, she carried it in and let the hand-carved wooden door to the piazza swing shut behind her. Dumping her things onto the nearest patio chair, she sat down on the chaise and looked at the envelope again. Taking a deep breath, she pulled the tab to open it and removed the contents.

A thick pouch of paperwork slid out, clamped together with a heavy-duty binder clip. Her eyes scanned the cover letter, but it was what she expected. Finn's first volley in the legal battle ahead. She could've saved him a lot of time if he'd just called her instead of running to his attorneys at the first word of a child.

Flipping through, she eyed the paragraph about the paternity test results—surprise, it was Finn's baby. Then she moved on to the topics of shared custody arrangements, monthly financial support, a trust fund for the baby, and even an offer to purchase and maintain a residence for them both. To say that Finn was being generous was an understatement. She was stunned by the numbers she was seeing. He wasn't a man to walk away from his responsibility, but was the kind willing to pay enough to keep everyone quiet and happy. This was more than she ever expected. And absolutely nothing she wanted.

Maybe she was stupid and naive to hope for more, but she did. Not just a weekend daddy and a big check for her child. She wanted a family. A real, legitimate family. If she had to choose her future husband from a catalog, no, Finn wouldn't be the one she would pick, but she had to play the hand Fate had dealt her.

Hearing her cell phone ringing inside her purse, Kat tossed aside the paperwork with disgust and reached for it. It wasn't a number she recognized, or even a local number, but she answered, figuring a telemarketer might be a welcome distraction.

"Hello?" she answered with a heavy sigh.

"Um, Katherine?" a man's voice asked with uncertainty. "Kat?"

"Yes?" It wasn't a telemarketer. They never called her Kat. Only her friends and family called her by that name. She pulled the phone away from her ear to look at the number again. It wasn't local. It wasn't even a US number, from the looks of it.

"This is Finn Steele," she heard, as she pressed the phone back against her ear.

"Oh."

That wasn't what she expected to say. Or what she'd planned to say once she finally got in touch with the father of her child, but that was what came out. "I got the love letter you sent."

"The *what*?"

"The offer from your attorneys."

"Oh." Finn chuckled nervously. "I was hoping

it hadn't arrived yet. I wanted to talk to you first and let you know it was coming, but my lawyer is more efficient than I expected for someone paid by the hour."

"I'm sure he has a standard template he uses for all his rich clients and their pregnant mistresses." Kat couldn't help the bitter tone from leeching into her voice. She even winced at the sound of it, compared to Finn's friendly, conversational tone. No matter what, being ugly to him wouldn't help matters. Slapping Sawyer certainly hadn't. "I'm sorry," she stated, when he didn't respond. "It's the pregnancy hormones. And calling me just as I was reading the legal paperwork didn't tip things in your favor."

"What's wrong with it? Patrick said he was going to put together a very generous offer."

"It was. Very generous. Maybe too generous, under the circumstances. I can't help but feel like you're trying to sweep us under the rug. You can't write a check and make this all go away, Finn. This isn't a fender bender. It's a child. Our child. And it deserves a family."

There was a long silence on the line. Kat was tempted to keep talking, but stopped herself. It was the truth and he needed to hear it, understand it, and respond accordingly. So she waited for him to answer.

"I'm sorry. You're right. You're not a dirty secret. You're carrying a Steele grandchild. It's not an ideal situation, but it's not the end of the world, either. I just wish I wasn't in China right now. There's only so much I can do from here. But I'm going to talk to my parents. I'll tell them everything tonight and I'm sure they'll be eager to meet you as soon as they can."

"You want me to meet your parents? Without you?"

"Yeah, sure. You'll be fine. You'll get to know everyone and by the time I get back stateside, I'm sure you'll feel better about having a family that accepts our child as one of their own."

That was nice, but that wasn't exactly what she had in mind. "I was actually thinking of something a little bit more legally binding on the family front, Finn."

"I can assure you that the offer my attorneys sent you is the best for everyone, Kat."

"Not for me, Finn. I want to get—"

"You don't want to marry me," he interrupted.

Kat was stunned into momentary silence by his abrupt response. She was expecting him to give her a reason why he couldn't or wouldn't marry her, not the other way around. "I don't?"

"No. Listen, you've spoken to my brother. I'm

sure he was all too eager to tell you about all my flaws. He revels in them."

"I'm not concerned with your flaws," Kat argued.

"You should be. There's a lot of them. I know that in your head getting married and raising this family together is the practical, responsible thing to do. But I am neither practical nor responsible. Ask anyone who has ever met me. Marrying me would…not be the fantasy you have in your mind."

She could hear Finn sigh on the other end of the line before he continued. "This isn't the old days where we have to marry to cover up the fact that we sinned together. I doubt many happy marriages resulted from that practice back then, and it wouldn't result in a happy marriage now. If I thought that I would be a good husband and father, I would get down on one knee the moment I saw you again. But I can't offer what I don't have. What I can offer you is support, and my last name for our child. He or she will be a Steele, and will be raised as such. You can meet my family and be as involved with them as you'd like. But believe me when I say you don't want to compound this mistake with marriage."

It was a good argument. And Finn sold it well. And if marriage hadn't been such a firm fixture in Kat's mind since she was a small child, she might even be swayed by his words. But what Finn didn't understand, what none of them understood, was what it was like to grow up with parents who weren't married. It wasn't the fifties then, and it still made her feel different. As though she wasn't good enough. Kat never wanted her child to feel like that. Especially just because the father was being selfish.

"Are you sure you're not just saying all this because you don't want to get married?" she countered.

"Of course I don't want to get married!" he shouted over the line. "That's one of the reasons I'll be so terrible at being a husband. Kat, I am not the marrying kind of guy. I've never even considered the possibility. I love the ladies too much to pick one for the rest of my life. I've always known this about myself, and that's why I've always tried to be very careful where contraception was concerned. I never wanted to put myself or a woman in this position, and until now I've been successful. I don't know why it happened this time, but I can't change it, or me. I'm saying this for your sake, for our child's sake and for my own sake. None of us will be happy if we get married."

"Let's table that discussion for now," Kat said. "What about being a father? Let's set aside talk of child support and trust funds and discuss what being a father really means to you. Do you intend to be involved?"

"Absolutely. I believe my lawyer submitted a request for visitation every other weekend, alternate holidays and a week during the summer. That seemed to be pretty standard."

Kat sighed. "And what about the rest of the time? What about school plays and ball games? Recitals, science projects? Playing in the park? Sitting up with him or her all night when our child has a fever and can't get comfortable?"

"To be honest, I didn't expect you to want me to be that involved. I'm willing to do as much or as little as is needed. I work long hours, and travel a lot, too. I may not be able to make every after-school game and class party. But if you really need me to be there, I will do what I can."

At this point, his words felt like a win to Kat. It wasn't all that she wanted, but it was a big step for their first talk. Maybe once he returned home from China, they could spend more time together. There was still a chance he might change his mind and want to be more involved in not only their child's life, but hers, too. She wouldn't give up hope yet.

"Look over the paperwork, Kat. It doesn't cover everything, but it does cover a lot. We can talk about it more in a few days. In the meantime, I'm going to talk to my parents. Keep an eye out for a mushroom cloud over Mount Pleasant. I'll talk to you soon."

Kat hung up the phone and leaned her head against the back of the seat. After everything that had happened the last few days with Sawyer and now with Finn, she was emotionally and physically exhausted. It didn't take much lately. The tiny human inside her seemed to sap her of any energy she might have. She wasn't sure how she was going to handle it when the baby got bigger, or worse, after it was born and mobile.

The idea of having a child alone was terrifying. It was a thought she hadn't really allowed herself to entertain. Every time the scary what-ifs crept into her mind, she would tell herself that Finn would marry her and they would be one big, happy family. But was she just lying to herself? If she accepted the fact that she was doing this on her own, would she be better prepared to face the eventuality?

Kat glanced down at the legal papers she'd set aside. Finn's attorneys had promised her a great deal of security. As much as money could buy. That was something. But Finn's money wouldn't hold her at night or get up and change the baby at 2:00 a.m. when she was too exhausted to get out of bed.

She tried to picture Finn doing just that. She

could see him in a pair of boxer shorts, clutching a small baby to his chest. Both he and the infant had the same golden-blond curls as he bent to kiss the baby on the top of the head. It was a touching image. One that nearly made her tear up at the thought. But as she let the fantasy play out in her mind, she knew one thing was different in this scenario.

It wasn't Finn holding her baby in her mind.

It was Sawyer.

Sawyer stood awkwardly on Kat's doorstep, holding a large box with a bow on it. He'd gotten the address from Finn's attorneys, but it felt weird to stand here on the piazza steps of her home with a gift. Unannounced. Like he was asking her to the prom or something. He suppressed that comparison lest the image of her in a slinky beaded dress completely derail why he was here today.

This visit wasn't about his brother. Or the District. Or his undeniable urge to see her again. And kiss her again. No. It was about his family.

He rang the doorbell, stopping to admire the intricate engravings on the front door. The edges were done in a Celtic knot design that ran all the way around, with leaves, acorns, chipmunks and other woodland creatures carved into the dark wood. It was incredible, and no doubt one of her pieces.

Kat opened the door, a look of confusion wrinkling her nose as she eyed him and the box in his arms. "Sawyer? What are you doing here?"

Considering he hadn't seen her since they kissed in her workshop and now he was at her home without prior warning, that was a valid question. To be honest, he hadn't called ahead because he thought she might tell him not to come. That was the smart thing to do. Let the lawyers handle the situation and stay far from the temptation of Kat McIntyre. And yet here he was, on a mission he'd volunteered for.

"I'm here today on official Steele family business," he said. At least that might ease any concerns she could have about him being here for less than altruistic reasons. He wasn't at her home to kiss her again. Although he'd have a hard time turning her down if she wanted him to. Kat was apparently the Achilles' heel he never knew he had until their lips touched that afternoon at the District. Since then, he'd thought of little else.

"What official business is that?" She crossed her arms over her chest and leaned against the door frame.

"Well, news of you and the baby has spread to the immediate family." Sawyer hadn't been at the house the night Finn called, so had heard the tale secondhand from Lena, their housekeeper. Apparently, they'd had to call the doctor, because his father had turned bright red as his blood pressure went through the roof. Sawyer wouldn't tell Kat that, though.

"Everyone is very excited to meet you and they don't want to wait until Finn gets home, so my parents have asked me to invite you to a little thing they're putting on this weekend at the house."

"A little thing?"

Sawyer knew well enough that nothing his parents ever did could be described as little. Perhaps in their mind a garden party for a hundred of their closest friends was an intimate get-together, but normal people knew better. "My grandmother is coming home. She's spent the last three years traveling around Europe after my grandfather passed away. I guess she finally got tired of Paris and has decided to come back to Charleston. They're throwing a welcome-home party for her Saturday afternoon and they'd like you to come."

He could tell by the look on Kat's face that she wasn't excited by the invitation. Some people dreamed of being invited to a Steele party. But some people weren't carrying the illegitimate child of the family's problem son. He imagined that, for someone in her position, a party like that would be akin to being dropped in a shark tank wearing a chum bikini. This might take some convincing.

"Can I come in?"

Kat nodded and stepped back to allow him up the stairs and inside the piazza. He followed her into the house, and as she shut the door and turned to face him, he held out the large box to her. "This is for you."

"What is it?" she asked cautiously.

Sawyer shrugged. "I think it's a dress. It's from my sister Jade, so I'm not entirely certain. She just told me to give it to you."

Kat accepted the box, but the line between her brows deepened with thought as she eyed the sizable package. "Why would she give me a dress? Or anything at all for that matter? We've never even met before."

"Well, that's true, but Jade is technically new to the family, too. I don't know if you follow the news, but she and my sister Morgan were switched at birth as part of some kidnapping and ransom scheme. Jade is my biological sister, but no one knew it until recently. When she heard about your situation, she told me she wanted to help out. She knows what it's like to walk into a room of Steeles as a stranger."

Kat carried the box over to the coffee table. "That's sweet of her. But why a dress? I have clothes. Is she worried I'm going to show up to this thing in cutoffs and flip-flops?"

"No, of course not. But she knows you're expecting. And I mentioned how you'd complained about your nice clothes not fitting at Morgan's wedding. Really, I don't know why. I didn't ask. She just gave me a box. It's her way of welcoming you to the family, I guess."

"I suppose I should be happy that someone is welcoming me," Kat muttered, as she opened the lid to expose the tissue-wrapped outfit inside.

It was coral-colored lace, and when she held it up, Sawyer could see why his sister had chosen it. It would flatter Kat's new curves nicely with its high waist, plunging V-neckline, and hem that would fall just above her knee. Her shapely calves would be on display all afternoon, and he couldn't complain about that. He was undoubtedly a leg man.

"This is beautiful," she said. "And just the right size. How did she know?"

He shrugged. He wouldn't even begin to guess what size a woman wore. It was a losing game for a man anyway, so he chose not to play. "She saw you hit me at the wedding reception and took a guess. She has an eye for clothes."

"I'll have to tell her thank-you when I see her

at the party." Kat folded the dress and placed it neatly back inside the box.

"So you're coming?"

Kat sighed and sat back on her sofa. "I don't suppose I can say no or I'll be starting off on the wrong foot with Finn's family. Your family," she added, with a wistful look in her eye he didn't understand. "I wish it wasn't such a big, public spectacle, though."

"That's better, really." Sawyer sat on the sofa beside her. "There will be a lot of people there and the focus won't be on you. It will be on Grandma Ingrid. You'll be able to mingle and meet people, but you won't be trapped in the dining room with the immediate family grilling you over dinner."

Sawyer had been witness to one such family dinner in recent memory. His older brother, Tom, had brought home a woman to meet the family. He'd seriously been considering proposing to her. But watching her melt to a puddle under the scrutiny had changed his brother's mind. If she couldn't handle dinner, she couldn't handle being a Steele.

"Okay, I guess. What time?"

"Three o'clock at the house."

Kat nodded and picked up her phone to put the information into her digital calendar. "Is there anything else I should know?" she asked.

"I'd recommend wearing shoes that won't sink into the lawn. And wear some good sunscreen and insect repellant. My parents have the yard sprayed, but it's still summer in Charleston."

Kat smiled and shook her head. "Thanks, but that's not exactly what I meant."

He was afraid of that. "What do you want to know?" he asked. "I'll answer you as honestly as I'm able to."

"Your parents... Finn told me he was going to tell them. Are they okay with this? I can't imagine they took the news well."

Sawyer sighed. "They didn't. At least at first. My family has always been very focused on their public image. They're getting better, though. I think my father has finally come to terms with the fact that we are all adults now, and the more he meddles in our lives, the worse it can make things."

Kat's lower lip trembled just slightly as she turned away and looked at the dress on the table. "So they hate me," she said matter-of-factly.

Sawyer wanted to reach out to her. To brush his thumb across her lip and kiss her until she forgot about his parents and what they might think. In the end, that mattered very little. Not as much as seeing her smile again. He compromised with himself and instead reached out to place a comforting hand on her denim-clad knee. "No. They don't hate you, Kat. They don't know you. But they want to get to know you and see what kind of person you are."

"They may not hate me, but they blame me for this. They think I'm just after their money and their name."

"Again, they don't know you. I'm sure they have their concerns, but they're polite enough not to confront you with them. Their future grandchild is at stake. They want to like you, I promise. Honestly, in this situation they blame Finn. I'm sure they're surprised it's taken this long for something like this to happen."

The frown line returned between her brows. It seemed to whenever he spoke about his brother. He understood her concern. She hadn't said anything to him about Finn, but he could tell that his twin's reputation bothered her. One night together wasn't enough time to decide if someone is going to be a good parent or partner.

"Just be yourself, Kat. Come and meet everyone. It will be fine. You'll get through Saturday and I'm sure it will be easier after that. My family isn't that scary."

"You're pretty scary." Kat gave him a shady bit of side eye and a knowing smirk as she said the words. It was enough to make him pull away his hand.

"I am. As you will soon learn, Morgan is the princess, Tom's the golden boy, Finn's the fuck-up and I'm the hard-ass." Sawyer stood and shoved his hands into his pockets. "Welcome to the family, Kat."

Five

The second time Kat drove up to the Steele mansion, the circumstances were very different. It had been only a few weeks and the live oak–lined drive with its dripping Spanish moss was just the same, but this time she had been invited. And hopefully, she wouldn't cause a scene.

There were already a lot of cars parked in the field when she pulled up and handed the keys of her Jeep to the valet. Another man directed her down a path along the side of the house to the backyard. She could hear a string quartet playing and the melody of voices and laughter in the distance.

But it wasn't until she rounded the corner of the house and caught a glimpse of the party that the wave of nerves hit her. She wasn't sure how many people she was expecting, but this was hardly a *little thing* Sawyer had invited her to. The event sprawled across the manicured lawn behind the house. A huge, white tent covered a portion of the tables and she could see a large buffet laid out in the shade.

There were more than a hundred people milling around in their garden party finery and flashy hats, with almost as many staff in white tuxedos catering to their every need.

As she stood at the edge of the crowd, trying to force herself to officially enter, one of the staff approached her with a tray of crystal flutes. "Would you care for some champagne, miss?"

Kat stopped herself from reaching out on impulse and dropped her hand to her stomach instead. Her baby belly was still little more than a bump, but the gown Jade had bought her for the party highlighted what she did have. "I'm not drinking."

"Of course, miss." The man snapped his fingers and another waiter appeared with a different tray of drinks. "The elder Mrs. Steele doesn't drink, so we also have sparkling cider and sparkling fruit waters available for guests."

Kat was surprised, but pleased. Alcohol was what she probably needed to calm her nerves, but at least she could have a crystal flute to hold, and feel like she belonged. She reached out and selected a glass of faintly pink bubbling water with a plump red strawberry wedged on the rim. "Thank you."

The waiters nodded and left, leaving Kat no choice but to finally move on. She slowly followed the trail toward the crowd, ignoring the drag of her feet, which felt almost as heavy as concrete. She knew it wasn't the shoes. If she allowed herself to turn and leave, she could probably sprint. She just didn't want to go to this party.

"Katherine?"

Kat wasn't used to people using her full name. Her mother was really the only one who ever called her Katherine. She stopped and turned her head toward the voice, seeing a stunning young blonde heading her direction. She immediately tensed. She didn't know who this woman was, but could tell in an instant that this was perhaps the most beautiful woman she'd ever seen in person.

Her hair was platinum blond, and she had big doe eyes and a wide grin, her fuchsia-colored lipstick matching her dress. She was tall, thin and elegant, moving with a swift grace in Kat's direction despite the four-inch heels she was wearing.

"You *are* Kat, aren't you?"

Kat took a breath and did her best to return the smile. "I am."

"I'm Jade, Finn's sister. I recognized you in the dress I sent over with Sawyer for the party."

With a sigh of relief, Kat felt the muscles in her shoulders start to unwind. At least she had one friendly face in the sea of strangers. "Oh! Thank you so much for sending this. You didn't have to, but it's lovely."

"Yes, I did have to. It fits you perfectly, I'm so glad. Asking Sawyer about your measurements was like asking a tiger how to prepare a five-course vegetarian meal."

Kat looked down to admire the coral lace and smiled. "I appreciate you thinking of me. Honestly, I'm not sure if I would've come today if you hadn't sent the dress over with Sawyer. I'm so nervous."

"I understand. The first time I met the Steeles, I was almost thirty years old. I was their biological daughter, and yet I'd never laid eyes on any of them, or them me. Seeing them face-to-face and finally learning the truth about our family and what happened was so stressful. But I don't regret it. Now I have two amazing families, four brothers and a sister of sorts that I adore."

"It's different for me," Kat replied, feeling her smile fade ever so slightly. "You were taken from them, but you belonged here. I'm an outsider who could be using their grandchild as a means of shoe-horning her way into the family fortune."

Jade narrowed her gaze at Kat for a moment. "Is that what you're doing?"

Kat shook her head. "No, but I wouldn't believe me if I were in their shoes. Sawyer is certainly suspicious enough of my motives."

"Sawyer is suspicious of everyone. That's just the way he is. Ignore him."

Kat bit her tongue, but she wanted to say that was easier said than done. The serious Steele twin had gotten under her skin. Whether he was accusing her of something terrible or looking at her with blatant desire in his eyes, Kat couldn't help but want to be nearer to him. She'd never had that happen with a man before. Being aggravated by and attracted to a man at the same time was infuriating and confusing. Never mind having all those thoughts about the wrong person.

"Have you met Grandmother yet?"

"I haven't met anyone. I just got here."

"Well then." Jade grinned. "Let's go find ourselves some Steeles." She reached out and took Kat's hand, leading her across the lawn to the tent.

It was probably just as well that Jade was virtually dragging her through the party, because Kat wasn't certain she could do it herself. The farther into the crowd they went, the more curious gazes she could feel upon her. No one knew who she was or why she was at such an exclusive event, she guessed. She wasn't really sure why she was there, either.

"Mother Patricia? Guess who I found loitering near the car lot."

Another pale blonde turned toward them and Kat would swear she was the spitting image of what Jade would look like in twenty-five years. They actually could've been confused as sisters. The woman took a moment to study Kat, and after her gaze fell on the slight curve of her stomach her dark eyes immediately shot back up to her face. "You must be Katherine," she said, with a smile that was warmer than expected, yet a little formal and stiff at the same time.

"Please call me Kat," she said, reaching out to shake the woman's hand.

"Kat, this is Patricia Steele, our mother."

Kat could've guessed that much without being told. "It's nice to meet you, Mrs. Steele."

Patricia looked around the crowd and frowned. "I think Trevor just slipped away into the house to talk business. He hates these dull affairs. Until he shows up again, I can introduce you to his mother, Ingrid. This party is in her honor. She's just returned to Charleston after several years in Europe."

Kat nodded blankly and let herself be carried along to meet someone else. She didn't expect what she found, however. Sitting in a chair near the stage was an older woman with the carriage of the queen of England. She was wearing a light pink suit dress with a matching blazer, white gloves and sensible white flats. There was a single strand of pearls around her throat and teardrop-shaped ones hanging from her ears. Her white hair was elegantly curled and coiffed, missing only a tiara to complete the look.

When the woman turned to look her way, Kat felt a surge of nerves worse than anything she'd felt before. This was the family matriarch, the guest of honor, and likely the one whose opinion would weigh the heaviest where Kat was concerned. Making a good impression was paramount.

"Mrs. Steele," the younger Mrs. Steele said. "I'd like to introduce you to Katherine McIntyre. This is Finn's lady friend."

The woman narrowed her dark brown eyes at Kat and smirked. "Judging by that little tummy, she's more than just his lady friend, Patricia." She turned away from her daughter-in-law to focus her full attention on Kat. "Come closer, dear. Have a seat beside me."

She patted the empty chair beside her with a gloved hand and Kat knew better than to decline. The older woman was no cookie-baking granny—she was sharp-tongued and quick-witted. Kat needed to stay on her toes with Finn and Sawyer's grandmother, she could tell.

"It's lovely to meet you, Mrs. Steele. I've been told you just returned from Europe? That sounds amazing. I've always wanted to travel more."

The older woman shrugged nonchalantly, as though she hadn't been globe-trotting for the last few years. "Sometimes you need to run away from home to get some perspective. Though most people don't wait until they're eighty to do it. Katherine, is it? Or Kate, perhaps?"

"Kat."

"Kat. I like it. I'm Ingrid. There's too many Mrs. and Miss Steeles around here. It gets confusing. So just call me Ingrid to keep things simple."

Kat nodded, noticing Patricia stiffen beside her. It made her wonder if she was allowed to call her mother-in-law by her first name.

"Why don't you run along, Patricia. I'm sure you have guests to tend to. I want to get to know this young lady better."

Patricia looked at Jade with a bit of concern, then pasted a smile on her face. "Of course. We will have plenty of time to spend with Kat. Call me if you need anything, ladies." She took Jade's arm and led her daughter to the other side of the tent, where some ladies in decorative hats were chatting.

Ingrid turned to Kat and placed a gentle hand on her knee. "Relax, dear. I know it's stressful, but I'm not going to bite. It's never easy being the wife of one of the Steele men. It's been over sixty years and I still remember the night Edward— that's Trevor's father—introduced me to his parents. It was nerve-racking to say the least, but I held my own. And so did Patricia. And so will you. Becoming Mrs. Steele is like taking on a new identity."

Her words were kind and reassuring, but Kat wondered why Ingrid was telling her this. Yes, she wanted to do the right thing and marry Finn, but she hadn't said as much to anyone aside from Finn himself. Then again, the family probably assumed that was what Kat would want: a diamond ring and a piece of the Steele pie for herself. That wasn't exactly the way she envisioned it.

"When my husband died three years ago," Ingrid continued, "I realized I didn't know who I was any longer. Who was Mrs. Steele without Mr. Steele? I was just some grandmother shuffling around the house having tea and waiting to die myself. That's why I left. I went to Europe to mourn Edward and find out who Ingrid was now. I went to London, to Barcelona, to Florence and finally to Paris. I sat on my balcony on the Île Saint-Louis overlooking the Seine and listened to the bells of Notre Dame cathedral ring every day. I sipped cafe crème, ate whatever I liked, and took long strolls down streets without knowing where I was headed. I found Ingrid again in Paris. And the night the cathedral burned, I decided it was time to come home."

Kat couldn't imagine living a life like that, but it sounded like the kind of thing that would feed an artist's soul. She wondered if Ingrid had some artistic talents, as well.

"It was time to come back to my family. And now I know why. I needed to come back here for you."

At that, Kat perked up in her chair. "For me?"

The older woman smiled and nodded. "Yes. As I said, it isn't an easy road to becoming Mrs. Steele, especially in your situation. People will talk, as though they have any room to judge someone else. You need someone on your side. The minute I laid eyes on you, I decided I was that person."

Kat's nose wrinkled and she took a nervous sip

of her drink. "Shouldn't you be on your family's side?" she asked, when she worked up the nerve.

"I am," Ingrid said with a curt nod. "They just don't know it yet."

Sawyer wasn't sure how Kat did it. He'd seen people nearly pass out from anxiety when meeting his grandmother. She didn't mince words, always speaking her mind whether she should or not. She also had an uncanny ability to see through people's bullshit. Her words, not his. Anyone approaching her with an ounce of haughtiness would be quickly cut down to size, his own mother included.

And yet, there Kat was at his grandmother's side. She'd been there almost all afternoon. The party was to welcome his grandmother home from Europe, and he was certain there were people anxious to speak with her, but Ingrid Steele simply didn't care. She seemed to be entranced by the young Miss McIntyre.

Sawyer knew exactly how she felt.

Leaning against one of the aluminum posts that held up the gigantic tent, Sawyer had watched over the two of them—Kat in particular—for quite a while. He'd argued with himself about why he was keeping such close tabs on his brother's lover. Of course, he told himself that he was waiting for the truth to come out about her and her motives.

If anyone could get to the bottom of Kat and what she was after, it would be Grandmother. And yet the two of them were chatting, laughing and nibbling on tea cakes like old friends.

In that case, Kat was either an incredibly skilled con artist or she was telling him the truth. Despite his suspicious nature, he hadn't found out anything about Kat that would raise a red flag. Jade's fiancé, Harley Dalton, owned a security and investigations firm and had personally done a background check on her. She came back squeaky clean. Probably even cleaner than Sawyer would.

She'd been orphaned in her late teens when her parents were killed in a car accident. She'd inherited a tidy sum from her parents' estates and insurance policies. From what he could tell, she'd left most of it invested and lived on the interest after buying her house. No police record. No bad debts. They couldn't even find an off-color social media post that could come back to haunt her.

Unless she'd suddenly decided to better her position by seducing and getting impregnated by the richest guy she could find, it was probably truly an accident, as she'd said. He hated to admit it, but all the evidence pointed to that outcome. Even Finn had mentioned that Kat was reluctant to accept any of the things his lawyers had offered her. If she was a scam artist, she was either terrible at it or positively diabolical.

Deep down, Sawyer knew she was innocent of the things he'd accused her of. Of course, once he stopped looking at her with suspicion, he couldn't help but look at her in a way that could only cause trouble for everyone involved.

"If I didn't know better, I'd say you were checking out that hot redhead with Grandmother."

Sawyer turned at the sound of his sister's voice. "That's just what Morgan would say if she were here, instead of on her honeymoon, gallivanting about."

Jade laughed. "Today, the role of the Steele daughter will be played by the understudy, Jade Nolan."

Sawyer wrapped his arm around her and tugged her close. "You're not an understudy. You originated the part for a short run before leaving the production for a gritty indie role."

"Cute. But don't change the subject." Jade tilted her chin in the direction of Ingrid and Kat. "Why are you over in a corner leering at Finn's baby mama?"

"I am not leering." Sawyer pulled away and crossed his arms over his chest. "I told Finn I would handle things for him and keep an eye on her until he got back from China."

"I don't think he intended for you to keep *that* good a watch on her. I suppose you can't help it, though. If you built a woman in a computer to your precise specifications it would come out Kat McIntyre."

Sawyer turned toward his sister with an irritated scowl. "You don't know what you're talking about."

Jade arched an eyebrow and nodded. "If you say so."

"Besides," he argued, "she's not available even if she was my type. She's with Finn."

"Do you really think so?" Jade looked over at Kat and narrowed her gaze in intense study. "I never pegged him for the settling-down type. Even with a baby in the mix. I don't imagine those two are going to ride off into the sunset together when he gets back from China."

Finn *wasn't* the settling-down type. But in this family people didn't always get to do what they wanted to. If they did, Morgan wouldn't have had to marry her husband, River, twice. "You never know what will happen. Something brought them together once, so it could happen again. And even if they just end up as co-parents or whatever…that doesn't mean there's a blank space in her life ready for me to occupy."

"Why don't you let her be the one to make that

decision?" Jade asked. "I've seen her look at you a few times this afternoon when you were distracted."

"What does that mean? I look exactly like Finn. She was probably just glancing at me and thinking about him. Or wondering if their baby will look like her or Finn. Even if she was staring me in the face, it'd be like she was looking at him."

"But she *wasn't* looking at him. She was looking at you. And appearances and birthdays aside, there's very little in common between the two of you."

Sawyer sighed heavily. "What's your point, baby sister?"

"*My point* is that if Kat had to choose between the two of you to be her husband and father to her child, the rebellious, irresponsible playboy probably wouldn't be her first choice. That's all." Jade gave Sawyer a pointed look and slowly strolled off in the direction of her fiancé.

Sawyer watched her head over to where Harley was standing and slip comfortably into his strong embrace. The man was huge, ex-navy, and intimidating enough to get a confession out of the toughest insurgent. And yet with Jade, he was like a big teddy bear. If she could turn a bad boy like that into marriage material, there might be hope for Finn and Kat.

That's what he should want, right? For things to work out between them? That was what Kat seemed to want. And it was best for the child to be with its father, after all.

But that wasn't what Sawyer wanted when he looked at Kat. When he saw her, all he could think about was kissing her again. That afternoon in her studio had haunted him. Her soft mouth against his, the curves of her body pressed into him, the taste of her lingering on his lips long after he'd left the District… He'd lived the moment over and over in his mind.

She'd pulled away, but he wasn't sure she'd really wanted to. Maybe Jade was right and Kat was interested in him, but she had a guilty conscience. Or the desire to do the right thing for her child outweighed everything else.

Sawyer knew about trying to do the right thing. Sometimes he thought he was the only one in his family who even attempted to do what was right. For all the good it did him. It didn't garner him any additional praise from his parents. No additional promotions or important assignments at work. It was almost like it was taken for granted that Sawyer would do the right thing, and he was ignored because of it.

Glancing back at Kat and his grandmother, he found Kat looking at him. Jade had been right about that, at least. When she realized she was caught, she smiled softly and wiggled her fingers at him in greeting.

No, kissing Kat hadn't been the right thing to do. But it had certainly felt right. Right enough that he wanted to do it again the moment he got her alone.

For once in his responsible life, Sawyer wanted to do the wrong thing.

Six

"Come on, you stupid Jeep!"

The valet had returned a few minutes ago, after attempting to bring her car around, and given her the bad news—her Jeep wouldn't start. With a groan of resignation, she'd taken the keys from him and trekked across the yard to where the vehicle was parked. Now she was sitting in it, hoping she had some sort of magic mojo the valet didn't, and the car would start.

So far, no luck.

This was an eventuality she'd been avoiding. The Jeep had been a present from her parents for her high school graduation. Even as she got older, there wasn't really any reason to replace the car. It was old and didn't have all the fancy features of newer ones, but it got her from A to B.

Since she found out she was pregnant, she'd been thinking more seriously about getting a new ride. One with doors, perhaps. It seemed as though her old Jeep was making the decision for her.

"Please. Just get me home tonight and I'll promise to sell you to an outdoorsy guy that will fix you up and drive you through all the mud puddles." Kat tried to turn the engine over again and found her attempts to negotiate had fallen on deaf ears. Because her Jeep didn't have ears.

With a whimper, she dropped her head onto the steering wheel in defeat. Why did it have to happen today? And here? Now the family she was trying to impress would have to see her junky old car get towed away from their multi-million-dollar estate. As though she wasn't already having enough trouble fitting in. She and Grandma Ingrid had hit it off, but most of the other people at the party had just regarded her from a distance.

When she went to fix a plate, all the ladies near the buffet had hushed until she was gone. It was quite juvenile for grown-ups, really. Kat wasn't used to being the subject of hot new gossip. And now they could be confident in believing her a gold digger. She didn't even have a functioning car—of course she was after Finn's money.

"Need some help?"

Kat shot to attention and turned to find Sawyer had silently crept up beside her car. "Did you go to ninja school or something?" she asked, pressing her hand to her rapidly beating heart.

"Morgan says I'd make a terrible spy. She insists I couldn't sneak up on her with a marching band going by. I didn't even try to slip out of the house when we were teenagers because I knew I'd get caught. So I'd say you were distracted."

"That's a word for it," she said. Turning away from him, she reached for her purse and rummaged around for her cell phone. She needed to call a wrecker. Most of the other guests were gone by now, so hopefully only the family would still be around when it showed up.

"It's awfully late," Sawyer said. "They're going to charge you extra to drive all the way out here on a weekend after eight. Why don't I give you a ride home? Then you can call someone to get the car in the morning, or on Monday."

Kat turned to him with a sigh. She certainly didn't want to sit out here in the humid summer air and get eaten by mosquitos while she waited. Then again, accepting a ride home from Sawyer seemed equally perilous. "I can call an Uber."

"Don't be silly. I can give you a ride. No one is going to want to come way out here to get you. Besides, I pass near your neighborhood on my way home, anyway."

She regarded him suspiciously for a moment, but when he offered his hand and stood there with an expectant look on his face, she finally gave in. "Okay."

He helped her out and only released her hand when he pointed to his car a couple yards away. "Don't act so put out. Most people would love to be chauffeured around in a brand-new car like mine. It still has the new-car smell."

Kat looked in that direction and spied a silver Audi SUV parked beside a bright yellow Porsche Boxster. She held her breath for a moment to see which one lit up when he pulled out his key fob. The lights on the Audi blinked on and off. She should've known better than to think that Sawyer would drive the flashier car. If she had learned more about him before that night at the aquarium, she would've realized she was with Finn, not Sawyer, when they left for a hotel and got into his bright red Ferrari.

Sawyer opened the passenger door and held it for her until she was inside. She sat patiently waiting as he came around to his side and started the car. It did have the new-car smell. It also looked as though it was fresh from the dealership. No travel mug in the cup holder, no crumbled-up receipts on the floor. It was immaculate.

"How long have you had this car?" she asked as they drove off the property.

"Two months, I think?"

"Oh," Kat said with surprise. "I was thinking more like a few days. This thing looks like it's hardly been driven."

"It's been driven. I just keep it pretty tidy."

"Is your place really tidy, too?"

She watched Sawyer frown at the windshield for a moment before he responded. "Maybe. But I have a cleaning service that comes in twice a week."

That sounded nice. She'd love to have one come in twice a month. Kat shook her head. "I bet they hardly do anything. I bet your underwear drawer is organized like a museum exhibit."

"My underwear is hardly museum quality," Sawyer said with a chuckle. "But I do have them rolled and stood on end as Marie Kondo suggests."

Kat rolled her eyes and relaxed back into the plush leather seat. "You need a little messy in your life."

"How's that?" he asked.

"You just seem very…straightlaced. Maybe you're trying to compensate for your brother or something, but you never seem to make a mis-

step. You need to loosen up. Even your grandmother agrees."

Sawyer turned to her with a confused arch of
his brow. "You were talking about me with my
grandmother?"

"Yes. She had a lot of nice things to say about
you, actually. I think you're her favorite."

"What makes you say that?"

"Just the way she talks about you. It seems like
she really wants you to find someone and settle
down. She wants you to find someone who makes
you happy, not just someone you think the family
will approve of, like your last few girls."

Kat watched Sawyer's knuckles tighten and
grow white as he gripped the steering wheel. "I
thought this afternoon was about my family getting to know you, not about Grandmother spilling
all the family gossip to you."

She shrugged and turned back to the road. "We
talked about me a lot, too. And about Finn. About
Jade and Morgan's situation. Ingrid really seemed
to take a liking to me for some reason. I don't
know why."

"Really?"

"What do you mean, really?" Kat turned toward
Sawyer as he slowed to a stop in front of her house.

He turned off his engine and looked at her. "My
grandmother enjoys the company of interesting

people. I don't know why you would think you aren't interesting enough to keep her attention. You're smart, you're easy to talk to, you're an artist. There's a lot of layers to you that I'm sure she would find fascinating. I certainly enjoy talking to you."

Kat noticed he said the last part a little more quietly than the rest. It was a curious admittance from a man who had at one time seemed adamant that she was some kind of crook out to fleece his family. "I enjoy talking to you, too," she admitted.

An awkward silence followed. With any other man in any other situation, Kat would've expected Sawyer to lean in and kiss her good-night. That was the natural progression of a conversation like that. She could sense the statically charged energy inside the car. Even with the air-conditioning on, she could feel the heat of his body nearby and smell the lingering scent of his cologne.

It was enough to make her want to slip off her seat belt and scoot closer to him. Judging by the blood racing hotly through her veins and the tingle that sizzled down her spine when he looked her way, it was clear that Kat wanted him to kiss her. And yet he hesitated. And she understood why.

Their attraction to each other was nothing more than mistaken identity combined with a cruel trick of chemistry. She needed to just thank him, get out of his car and go into her house. She needed to look at her finances and start thinking about buying a new car, not about Sawyer and the way his blazer clung to his broad shoulders. Or the way the deep brown of his eyes reminded her of decadent dark chocolate.

Yes, that was what she needed to do. With a surge of self-control, she reached for the door handle and turned to say goodbye. "Would you like to come in for some coffee or something?" she said, instead of good-night or thanks for the ride.

The words slipped from her lips before she could stop herself. Why would she invite Sawyer into her house? The last time they'd spent any real time alone, they'd ended up kissing, and that was in public at her studio. What would happen late on a Saturday night at her house? With no one there to interrupt or know what was happening inside?

Her belly clenched as she awaited his answer.

"I'd like that."

A surge of excitement and a good dose of worry washed over her. Kat was about to find out exactly what would happen if they were alone again. And deep inside, she couldn't wait.

What are you doing? What are you doing?
Every step Sawyer took up the path to Kat's piazza raised a chorus of doubts in his mind. He

followed her inside, knowing full well that he was heading into dangerous territory.

It's just coffee, he told himself, but he knew that was a lie even as the thought entered his mind. If he crossed that threshold into Kat's home, it was like the point of no return. He already ached to kiss her. It had taken everything he had on the ride back not to reach over and cup her bare knee with his hand. He wanted to stroke the smooth skin he'd been eyeing all afternoon.

It was stupid. It was reckless. It was everything Sawyer typically looked upon with disapproval. And yet he couldn't help himself. He felt a bit like Finn, doing what he wanted without thinking about what others thought.

Inside her house, he watched Kat set down her things and kick off her heels with a sigh of relief. "That's the best thing to happen to me all day," she said with a soft smile. "Make yourself at home. I'm going to make some coffee."

He watched her disappear into the kitchen as he happily shrugged out of his blazer and tossed it over the back of a chair. Then he set about checking out more of Kat's place. He had been here before, when he'd delivered the dress from Jade, but he'd been too stressed out to pay much attention to his surroundings then. Now, with her in the other room, he was able to walk around and take in the place Kat called home.

The first thing he noticed was the collection of wood carvings around the living room. He recognized them as similar in style to some of her projects at her studio. There was a tall, narrow carving of a mermaid reaching toward the surface of the water, a couple embracing as the wind twirled her hair around them, and Kat's coffee table was an oval sheet of glass resting on the back of a green sea turtle. She really was a talented artist.

The piece that didn't seem to fit in was a large canvas painting above the sofa. It was a chaotic mash of colors that up close seemed like a mess, but from far away, you could see a little girl in a yellow slicker splashing in a rain puddle. He looked at the signature and recognized the name from Kat's background check. It was by her mother, Astrid Elliott. When he'd first read the name, it had sounded familiar, but now that he saw one of her pieces in front of him, he made the connection. Astrid had been a successful artist when she was alive, with the price of her works skyrocketing after her death. He'd even seen one of her pieces in the museum downtown.

On the fireplace mantel, he saw a framed family portrait that had to have been taken not long before the accident that killed both Astrid and Brent

McIntyre, Kat's father. Kat looked like a younger, happier version of the woman he knew, surrounded by the parents who loved her.

He noticed it was the only picture around the house. There was nothing more recent. He supposed that was because she didn't want to have pictures taken of herself alone. It seemed like a depressing thing to do, although the idea had never occurred to him until now. He'd always had more family than he knew what to do with. Lately, he'd gained a sister and two new brothers-in-law. He didn't know what it would be like to be alone in the world the way Kat was.

"How do you take your coffee?" Kat asked, as she came into the room with two mugs on a small tray.

"Black, normally, but it's too late for that. Cream, no sugar, or I'll be up all night."

Kat looked at him curiously for a moment, the curve of her mouth inching upward in an amused expression before she nodded and set the tray down on the coffee table. Thinking over his words in the current context of being alone in her house late at night, he could see why. Coffee or not, he might very well be up all night. *God*, he wanted to be up all night.

He was about to sit down on the sofa when he noticed her fidgeting in her lace dress. "Would you like to change out of your party clothes? You seem uncomfortable."

"Yes," she said with a relieved sigh, as she poured cream into his coffee and then straightened. "This lace has gotten itchier as the night goes on. I just hope I can get ahold of the zipper."

"I can get that for you," Sawyer offered.

Kat's gaze fixed on his for a moment. It seemed as though neither of them took a breath the entire time as she thought over his helpful suggestion and what could come of it. "Okay," she said at last.

Kat swooped her long red hair up off her neck to expose the zipper, and turned her back to him.

Sawyer's hands were almost trembling as he reached out to grasp the tab and hold the fabric taut. He tugged down, separating the teeth and exposing more and more of Kat's bare skin as he went. His fingertips brushed over the clasp of her pale pink bra before they continued down to the curve of her back. The zipper stopped there, just where the top of her panties would be visible. But they weren't.

"Did you go commando to my grandmother's garden party?" Sawyer managed to ask, his mouth suddenly as dry as sand.

Kat chuckled and swept her hair over her shoulder as she turned to him. "I had to. This dress showed panty lines pretty badly and I've never really been a fan of thongs."

The smile faded slowly from her face when she looked him in the eye. He wasn't sure what she saw there, but he was certain every feeling he was trying to hide was visible if she peered hard enough. He was usually good at disguising his feelings, but that was because he rarely had any. Now, standing here with her dress about to slip from her shoulders, he was overwhelmed with feelings like never before.

Without saying a word, Sawyer reached out and caught the neckline of her dress where it rested across her skin. He heard Kat's breath catch in her throat as he pulled at the coral fabric. It slipped off her shoulder, the weight of the dress pulling it from her other shoulder, as well. Kat didn't try to stop it as it slid down her body and pooled at her bare feet.

Sawyer swallowed hard as his gaze raked across Kat's virtually naked body. When she finally did move, it wasn't to grab her dress or cover herself. She reached behind her back and unfastened her bra. In a moment, it fell to the floor with her dress, leaving nothing but the red waves of her hair to cover any of her body from him.

He let out a ragged breath as he studied her pale, creamy skin. He was drawn to her full breasts and the hardened peach nipples that seemed to reach out to him, begging him to touch them. He wanted to. It was wrong, but he wanted to. He was conflicted enough that he was frozen on the spot, unable to leave and unable to pursue her.

Instead, Kat closed the gap between them. She stepped gingerly out of her dress and stopped just short of having her nipples graze the cotton of his dress shirt. "Don't you want to touch me, Sawyer?" she asked.

Hearing her specifically say his name, not his brother's, lit a fire deep inside his belly. This wasn't just a case of mistaken identity. She wanted *him*. In this moment, naked and vulnerable in front of him, she wanted Sawyer to touch her, and he was desperate to give her what she needed.

"More than anything," he admitted, and he meant it. He couldn't remember another woman in his life who had gotten under his skin, or taken over his thoughts, the way Kat had.

"Then touch me. Please. I want you to."

She wanted this. He wanted this. In that moment, Sawyer decided that nothing else mattered. He had to have Kat or he was going to make himself crazy with unfulfilled desire. He would regret not taking the chance, just as he would probably regret sleeping with her, so he might as well do what he wanted to in the heat of the moment.

Reaching out, he cupped one breast in his hand. Kat's head tipped back and her eyes closed as she savored the sensation. Her skin was soft as silk as his thumb traced over it and then teased the taut peak that pressed insistently into his palm.

With his other hand, Sawyer reached around the back of her neck, weaving his fingers through her hair and pulling her mouth up to meet his. She opened herself to him, moaning softly with pleasure as his tongue grazed hers. He drank her in, enjoying the lingering taste of strawberries on her lips from the flavored seltzers she'd sipped all afternoon.

He felt her fingers at his throat and pulled away from her mouth long enough for Kat to tug his tie loose and throw it onto the floor. She unfastened the top button of his shirt, which was always his favorite moment of the day. He supposed it was like Kat kicking off her uncomfortable shoes. He sighed in relief, and was about to dip his head down to taste her breasts when Kat pressed insistently on his chest, forcing him backward until his calves met with the couch behind him.

She pushed him back onto the sofa and crawled onto his lap to sit astride him. Her fingers worked feverishly to unbutton his dress shirt and push the fabric out of her way. Sawyer's hands gripped the flesh of her hips as she dragged her nails through his chest hair to his belly, then unfastened his belt.

Kat rose up on her knees long enough to let him slide his pants down his thighs, then she slowly, deliberately, lowered herself onto him.

Sawyer groaned against her breasts as he wrapped his arms around her and pulled her close to him. He held her still for a moment once she was fully seated, and squeezed his eyes tightly shut. He wanted to savor every moment, every feeling, because this probably wouldn't ever happen again. Soon they would come to their senses and realize how stupid they were, but right now, right this very second, he was going to enjoy every delicious sensation.

After a moment of stillness, Kat ran her fingers through the curls on the top of his head and gripped a fistful. Gently, she pulled back, until Sawyer had no choice but to look into her bewitching green eyes. Then she eased up and sank down on him a second time. Moving slowly at first, Sawyer leaned back and enjoyed the view of his redheaded hellcat taking control. This was the woman who'd slapped him hard across the face at his sister's wedding. The one who had called him daily and tried to track him down to get her way over the artist community. She was feisty. Sexy as hell. Kat was unlike any woman he'd ever been with before.

The slow burn she was building was teetering on the edge of torture. He wanted more and he decided it was time to turn the intensity up a notch. Sawyer reached out and cupped her hips to hold her steady. She braced her arms on his shoulders, letting her breasts sway tantalizingly just out of his mouth's reach. Then he planted his feet firmly on the floor and thrust up into her.

Sawyer watched Kat's expression as he moved hard and fast inside her. Her emotions shifted from surprise to delight, then the tense, almost pained look of a woman on the verge of undoing. He slowed temporarily, reaching between them to allow his fingers to stroke her center. Kat's mouth fell open, her eyes closing as she rocked with him to her climax. And then, once her first cry escaped her throat, he gripped her hips and thrust hard into her again until they were both satisfied and spent.

Kat collapsed against him in exhaustion and he was happy to catch her as she melted into him. She buried her face in his neck, with her hair cascading over his chest and shoulders. He was content to wrap his arms around her and hold her close as their heartbeats and breaths slowed back to normal.

So this is what it was like to do what you wanted to do. Sawyer had to admit it was exhilarating to take a page from his twin's book, damn the consequences. True, he might rot in hell for sleeping with the woman having his brother's child, but he just didn't care. Tonight was worth it.

And he couldn't wait to have her again.

Seven

Kat woke up late. Later than she'd let herself sleep in a long time. Of course, she had been up late with Sawyer. After their encounter on the couch, they'd finally had their cooling coffee, then moved to the bedroom to make love again.

And again.

Now, she was afraid to open her eyes to the light of morning and face reality. As long as she stayed right where she was, she could revel in last night without pondering the consequences.

It had been amazing. She wasn't ashamed to admit it. While Finn and Sawyer might look alike,

they were day and night when it came to the bedroom. Finn had the playboy reputation and an adventurous spirit, but she preferred Sawyer's style.
He was more serious, but also more thoughtful.
She'd never had a man focus so much on her
needs in bed. Kat had lost count of how many
times she'd come undone under his expert touch.
It seemed like anything less would've been a fail-
ure on his part.

Things with Finn had been…fine. He was a little wilder than what she was used to. She'd had a
good time. But somehow it didn't compare when
it came to intimacy, which was what she found
she really craved.

It made her wish more than anything that it had
really been Sawyer, not Finn, who she'd met that
night at the award ceremony. Somehow it seemed
like having his baby would be easier. She could
envision them actually having a future together
where they might be happy. With Finn, she got
the feeling she and the baby were just going to be
a stone around his neck.

Kat ran her hand across the mattress, and when
she found it empty and cold, she pried one eye
open. Sawyer was gone. Long gone, by the feel
of it.

It was a stark reminder that she wasn't having
his child. And she wasn't living some fairy tale.

With a groan, Kat pushed herself up out of bed and clutched the sheets to her chest. She almost felt hungover despite not having a drop to drink. She supposed she was love drunk and still feeling the aftereffects.

"A fine punishment, and duly deserved," she said aloud as she swung her legs out of bed. She really needed to get her priorities in line. There wasn't much sense in sleeping with one twin while wanting to marry the other. At the very least, it didn't help matters. Finn wasn't a model of monogamy, of that she was sure, but she didn't think he'd take kindly to knowing that she and his brother were having sex while she waited for him to return from China.

That was why no one would ever know. Kat would never speak of it. And it certainly wouldn't happen again. It had been an amazing night. One that was hard to regret. But she couldn't let her desires compromise her child's future.

She reached for her floral silk robe from the hook in her closet and wrapped it around herself before stumbling down the stairs to the kitchen. She half expected to see Sawyer sitting there, smugly drinking a cup of coffee, but the house was silent and still.

Which was why the loud beeping of a tow truck outside caught her attention so easily. Realizing that Sawyer must've had her Jeep towed to the house, she slipped into a pair of flip-flops and went out to the piazza to see what was happening.

There, a tow truck was unloading what looked like some kind of luxury SUV into her driveway. The cherry-red vehicle was beautiful, but definitely not hers.

Great. They'd gotten the cars mixed up. Her Jeep was probably getting dropped at some rich guy's yard in Mount Pleasant, where they were about to throw a fit.

With a groan of irritation, Kat tightened the belt on her robe and pushed through the heavy wooden door to flag down the tow truck driver. "Hey!" she shouted, waving her arms at the guy in the cab.

Finally the man noticed her and stopped what he was doing. "Yeah?"

"What are you doing? This isn't my car. You've got the wrong car or the wrong house."

The man turned from the window and picked up a clipboard to read the pages there. "Are you Katherine McIntyre?"

"Yes."

"Then I've got the right house and the right person." He went to hit the lever to continue lowering the SUV off the truck.

"No, this isn't right. This isn't my car. I drive a Jeep. A broken-down, dark green, rusty Jeep

Wrangler." She turned to the car halfway in her driveway. She could see now that it was a brand-new Lexus SUV. It wasn't even close to the right car. In her dreams.

"Listen, lady. I don't know anything about an old Jeep. All I know is that I was supposed to bring this vehicle from the dealership to this address and give the keys to you."

"On whose authority?"

The man rolled his eyes. He'd probably never had someone fight so hard against receiving a car. He looked down at the paper again. "Looks like a Mr. Steele had it sent. If you don't want the car, take it up with him. But I've got to deliver it. That's my job."

Before Kat could open her mouth to ask which Mr. Steele had sent it, he flipped the switch again and the cable lowered the SUV the rest of the way to the ground. The man finally climbed down from the cab and busied himself unhooking things and getting everything set up so he could leave. Then he raised the flatbed back into position and walked over to where she was waiting.

"Sign here," he said.

She was too tired to fight with him. She signed the paperwork, which drew an audible sigh of relief from the driver. Then he handed over a pair of key fobs.

"There are worse things than waking up to a new Lexus," he pointed out. "Have a nice day," he added, before crawling back into his cab and disappearing down the street.

Kat looked at the keys in her hand in disbelief, then slowly made her way over to the SUV. It was beautiful, with sporty lines and elegant chrome details. It had to be the latest model, with top-of-the-line trim features. The interior had red-and-black leather seats and a shiny polished wood-and-leather dashboard. It made her old Jeep look like it was made from papier-mâché or Tinkertoys or something.

It was exactly the kind of car she would have chosen for herself if she could've had any car in the whole world. Each detail, from the sunroof to the wheels, was perfect.

But she couldn't accept a gift like this. Not from Finn and certainly not from Sawyer.

Kat reluctantly walked back into her house and hunted down her phone from where she'd left it the night before. There, on her screen, was a text from Sawyer, answering her question at last.

Do you like it?

Kat rolled her eyes and shook her head before texting back. Of course I like it, she responded. But I can't accept it.

Her phone rang precisely five seconds later,

with Sawyer's number coming up on the screen. "Come get your car," she answered without saying hello.

"Good morning to you, too," he said in an irritatingly chipper voice. He knew full well how she would react to a gift like that and he seemed to be reveling in it.

"Good morning, Sawyer. Now will you please tell me why there's a brand-new Lexus in my driveway? Where is my Jeep?"

"Your Jeep is at the repair shop. I had it towed there early this morning. The guy took a look at it and said it's on its last legs. The starter has gone out, which is why it won't turn over, but he didn't feel right charging you to fix that because the whole engine would need to be rebuilt before too long, anyway. I can't have you stranded on the side of the road, pregnant and at the mercy of random bystanders."

Kat had been afraid that the news about her Jeep wouldn't be good, but this was even worse than she'd expected. "And so naturally, you bought me a new car instead?"

"Naturally." She could almost hear his smug grin in his voice.

"Sawyer…" Kat said in a stern tone.

"Hear me out," Sawyer argued. "You need a new car."

"That may be true, but it doesn't mean that you need to sweep in and buy one for me. If the Jeep is DOA, then I'll go get something else. You buying it after last night makes it feel like some sort of thank-you-for-the-sex gift."

Sawyer laughed over the phone line. It was one of the first times she'd ever heard him really, truly laugh. She liked the sound of it and wished she was with him in person to see if his eyes lit up or his dimple was on display. Finally, the laughter faded. "Do you really think I give cars to all the women I sleep with?"

"Well, no..."

"That would be an expensive habit, even for me, Kat. The truth is that yours isn't safe for you to drive and it certainly won't be safe to take my new niece or nephew around town, either. My brother asked me to keep an eye on things until he can get back, and in my opinion, the best thing I could do is get you a safe vehicle to drive."

While Kat was relieved it wasn't a morning-after gift, she still couldn't take something like that from him. Or from anyone. Even from Finn and his team of bribing attorneys, although they'd offered her everything but a car in their settlement package. "I can't accept this, Sawyer."

"That's a shame, since you currently have nothing else to drive. I can tell the mechanic to try and get your Jeep running, but it won't be a quick fix. I hope you don't have anything you need to do the next few days."

Kat sighed. "I actually have a doctor's appointment on Tuesday. Not to mention going to the District to work."

"Well, there's no way your car will be ready that soon. The guy only took it in today as a favor to me. How about this? Since you need a car to get around, drive the Lexus for a couple of days. I'll see what he can do with your Jeep. If he can get it running, I will take the Lexus off your hands. Maybe I'll give it to Morgan for her birthday."

Kat was more suspicious of this than anything. He'd backed down quicker than she expected. "Are you serious?"

"Absolutely. Red isn't really Morgan's color, but I think she'll like it."

"Why not just return it to the dealership, and I'll get a rental car?"

"I got too good a deal on it. If you don't want it, fine, but someone is getting a new Lexus. There's no sense paying for a rental car, too, when it's sitting there in your driveway."

"Okay," Kat said reluctantly. "Is this why you crept out of my bed at dawn?"

"I hardly crept out at dawn. It was eight thirty

and you were out like a light. I hated to wake you up, so I let you sleep."

That made Kat feel a little better, although as she looked down at the key fobs in her hand, she couldn't help but think that Sawyer would get his way where the car was concerned. Where everything was concerned, actually. No matter how much time they spent together, she never seemed to be able to pin him down to talk about the District. There were parties and family members and new cars to distract her, and she was running out of time.

"I'm going to talk to the guy about your Jeep and I'll give you a call back later, okay?"

"All right."

"Oh, and before I forget, do you have plans for the Fourth of July?"

Kat didn't need to look at her calendar to know she didn't. She figured she'd be working at the District, like she always was. They got higher than average foot traffic on holidays. Still, she liked the idea of seeing Sawyer again that soon. "I don't think so."

"Oh, good. Grandmother wanted me to invite you to the family Fourth of July party."

Kat tried to swallow her disappointment that it was Ingrid, not Sawyer, who wanted to see her again. At least she hadn't embarrassed herself too badly with the family if they'd invited her to another gathering. "Another party?" Kat asked. Her toes still hurt from the last one.

"This one is different. Just the immediate family cruising the harbor to watch fireworks from our yacht."

Kat cringed at the way Sawyer could talk about the family yacht as though that's what everyone did on a summer holiday. "I'll think about it," she said.

"I'll tell Grandmother Ingrid you said yes, then."

Before Kat could argue, the call ended and she found herself staring at her phone, dumbfounded. She certainly hadn't intended to get this involved with the Steele family, but now that she was, they were turning into a handful.

It was a nice change of pace from being alone.

"Come on back, Mr. Steele. Ms. McIntyre is already in the exam room, but the doctor is still with another patient."

Sawyer smiled and nodded to the nurse as she knocked gently on the door and then opened it to let him inside.

"Guess who's here?" the nurse said brightly. "Daddy was able to make the appointment, after all!"

Sawyer saw Kat whip her head around to where he was standing in the doorway. Her jaw clenched, but she didn't bother to argue with the nurse, or have him tossed and cause a scene.

"Great," she said flatly.

Once the nurse slipped back out the door, Kat's smile faded. "What exactly do you think you're doing, crashing my prenatal appointment?"

Sawyer shrugged and settled into the guest chair. "My brother told me to keep an eye on things. I'm sure he would want to be at this appointment if he were here, so I thought I'd pop in and pass any news along to him."

"So you just told them you were the father and they let you in?"

"Yes and no," he admitted. "I was waiting patiently in the lobby for you to finish. They approached and asked if I was the father and if I wanted to come back to see the ultrasound and get the lab results, so I said yes. It's not like they'll ever know me from Finn, anyway."

"I'll know." Kat fidgeted with her uncomfortable-looking paper gown.

"It's a little late to act shy around me," Sawyer said. "I've seen all this, and recently."

"This is different." Kat crossed her arms over her chest and twisted her lips in irritation.

Sawyer sat back in his seat and looked around.

He'd never been in a gynecologist's office before. There were big posters on the walls with drawings that reminded him of fifth grade health class, and the exam table had handles coming out the ends like a motorcycle. "What are these?" he asked.

Kat rolled her eyes. "Stirrups."

"Like for a horse?"

"Not exactly, but my feet do go in them. It's for the…exam."

Oh. Yeah, he'd definitely never been in one of these offices before. Or given much thought to what actually happened in them.

He was second-guessing his decision to crash the appointment when a quick rap at the door disrupted their conversation, and a shorter man in a white lab coat rushed in. "Hey, everyone, how's it going today?"

"Hey, Dr. Wheeler."

He shook Kat's hand and turned around to face Sawyer. "Dad? Friend? Moral support?"

"All of the above," he said.

"Okay, great," Dr. Wheeler said without missing a beat. He sat down on his little rolling stool and flipped open the medical file he'd come in with. "So the results on all the tests from your initial appointment look normal. No concerns there. Are you taking your prenatal vitamins?"

"Yes."

"Good. Any problems so far? Nausea? Tenderness? Spotting?" The doctor stood up and guided Kat back onto the table. Sawyer heard her respond, but at that point he checked out. He hadn't fully comprehended what he was walking into today and realized now that he didn't want to see the man behind the curtain, so to speak.

He let his gaze drop to his lap and tried not to think about what that man was doing to Kat. The next thing he knew the lights were dimming in the room and the doctor was spraying gel across Kat's bare stomach.

"We're going to take some pictures and I'm going to try to get a heartbeat on the Doppler. Hopefully we can get a good look at the little guy today."

"It's a boy?" Sawyer asked, perking up from his stupor.

The doctor smiled and shook his head. "We actually haven't talked about that yet. I do have a preliminary result from the NIPT test, if you would like to know. It's 90 percent accurate, but I wouldn't go painting any rooms until after we do the gender confirmation ultrasound at twenty weeks. Maybe we can see something today, but that depends on the baby and how cooperative she or he is feeling."

"I would like to know the test results," Kat said.

"Sure thing." The doctor picked up the folder and flipped to a page filled with lab results numbers. "Well, it looks to me like you guys *should* be expecting a little girl."

Kat brought her hand up to her mouth to stifle a soft cry. Sawyer wanted to rush to her side and share in the excitement, but it felt like intruding on someone else's moment. It wasn't his baby or his news, despite what he'd told them in the lobby earlier.

"My sisters are going to be thrilled," he said instead, with a reassuring nod to Kat. "And Mom and Grandma Ingrid, too. Once you know for certain you're going to be smothered in a sea of ruffled, pink baby clothes."

Kat laughed and he saw a shimmer of happy tears in her green eyes. He reached out and took her hand, squeezing it gently. He might not be the father, but until Finn got home, he would do what he could to support her through this.

Her gaze met his and she smiled. "Thank you for being here," she said. "I didn't realize I didn't want to be alone for this moment until right now."

He squeezed her hand again and they both turned their attention to the grainy image on the monitor. Dr. Wheeler moved the wand back and forth across her stomach while he searched the darkness for the tiny baby inside.

"Here we go. Hello, precious one."

Sawyer narrowed his gaze at the monitor, trying to make sense of what he was seeing. Then suddenly the profile of the baby came into focus and he felt the emotion of the moment hit him like a punch to his midsection.

He could see every little detail of her face, her little nose and mouth, and her hands balled up in front of her. He could see the curve of her spine and her legs drawn up to her tummy. The beating of her heart was visible, although they couldn't quite hear it over the static.

The doctor hit the keyboard repeatedly, capturing shot after shot of the baby, and then moving the wand to a different location for a new angle. At one point, he pointed out something completely indiscernible and said, "I'd say this is a girl for sure." He typed it on the screen, pointing out some blurry spots, and printed out another image. "You can go ahead and paint."

Then the doctor focused on the tiny fluttering heart on the screen and suddenly the room was filled with the rapid *wub-wub* sound of the baby's heartbeat.

Through it all, Sawyer held Kat's hand, fully enthralled in the moment as though this was his little girl on the screen, whose heartbeat he was hearing for the first time. His brother had screwed up a lot in his life, but Sawyer couldn't help but feel this wasn't just Finn's latest mistake. This might be the first thing Finn had gotten right.

He also felt an incredible sense of jealousy. He had no right to, really. I wasn't as though he'd been pining for a family of his own—far from it, actually. But somehow knowing that a simple twist of fate had put this woman in Finn's path instead of his own bothered him.

Kat. This baby girl. It was supposed to be his. Kat had come to that party looking for him, not Finn. If he hadn't been feeling poorly that night he would've been the one to meet her. Maybe he wouldn't have whisked her off to a hotel the way Finn did, but he couldn't help but think he would've asked her to dinner. And then more. And in time, maybe they would've been sharing this moment together over their child.

Finn hadn't just taken his Jet Ski and played pretend that night. It was as though his twin had stolen his whole future when he put on that name tag.

Eight

"Can I take you to lunch?"

Kat seemed surprised by his offer as they walked out of her doctor's building. "Don't you need to work or something?"

Sawyer frowned. "You sound like my dad. Come on, I'll take you wherever you want to go. Have you started having any weird food cravings yet?"

"I don't know, Sawyer." She seemed uncharacteristically uncomfortable with him. It felt odd to him after the moment they'd just shared. "I probably shouldn't."

Sawyer stopped and shoved his hands into his pockets. "Is something wrong?"

Kat squirmed beneath his gaze, adjusting her purse on her shoulder. His feisty hellcat seemed very out of her element at the moment. "I guess I'm just... I'm just thinking that maybe we shouldn't spend so much time together."

He wasn't sure why, but the words seemed to strike him in a tender spot. Maybe he was reading things wrong, but he thought they were having a good time together. Some could say too good of a time if they took Saturday night into consideration. And he'd bought her an expensive car that would raise eyebrows with his family if they knew about it. But he didn't care about any of that.

He'd done it because it felt like the right thing to do. Finn certainly wasn't going to show up and take care of her the way she deserved to be cared for. He wasn't going to go to doctor's checkups and worry about whether she had a safe vehicle to get around town. Being thousands of miles away was a convenient excuse, but if Finn were in Charleston this very moment, he still wouldn't be standing on this sidewalk beside Kat.

He'd asked Sawyer to handle things while he was gone, and Sawyer had gone over and above the call of duty. But Kat deserved someone who would do that for her. Being the go-between put Sawyer in a position he didn't expect to be in: one where he was starting to have feelings for the last woman and child on Earth that he should. They weren't serious feelings. But it was the closest thing to affection he'd felt for anyone since his breakup with Mira, and Kat's rebuff stung a little more than he expected it to.

"It's just lunch," he said. "I recommend keeping your clothes on for that, if you're concerned about us crossing the line again."

Kat bit at her lip and tucked a stray strand of auburn hair behind her ear. She had it in a messy bun today, but the breeze had liberated just enough to curve along the edge of her face. It softened the look, in his opinion, but it seemed to be irritating Kat. As did Sawyer's mere presence at the moment.

"Lunch. Just lunch," she finally agreed. "I guess we need to talk, anyway."

Sawyer ignored her ominous addition and instead pointed out a restaurant across the street touting modern Southern fare. The Charleston foodie scene was booming with little spots like this in the last few years. "How do you feel about that place?" he asked.

"That's fine."

They crossed the road together and went inside the restaurant, which was pretty busy considering it was on the late side for lunch. The hostess took them to a booth near the window and they settled in. The waiter brought them glasses of water and a basket of fried corn fritters with a spicy honey dipping sauce, before stepping away to let them look over the menu.

Sawyer decided on a burger with bacon, pimento cheese and a fried green tomato on it. Kat chose a salad with diced fried chicken, candied pecans and dried cranberries.

"Sawyer, before I say anything else, I want to thank you for being there today. It was unexpected, but at the same time, it was nice to have someone to share that moment."

"You're welcome." He got the feeling this was going to be the nicest part of this conversation. She had that worry line between her brows and that was never good.

"That said, I feel like we need to talk about the other night," she said, once the waiter disappeared.

Here it comes, Sawyer thought. He'd insisted on this lunch and now he was about to be dumped by a woman he wasn't even dating. "What about it?" he said, playing coy. He reached for a fritter and shoved it nonchalantly into his mouth. If she wanted to backpedal on everything they'd shared, he certainly wasn't going to act like it was one of the greatest nights of his life and be at a disadvantage with her.

When he stripped the encounter down to the core, it was just sex. Great sex, but only sex. No promises, no emotional entanglements. They shouldn't need to talk about it unless one of them saw it as more than that. It piqued Sawyer's attention that Kat seemed to think it meant something.

"Well, it's just you left so early and then the stuff happened with the car and we just never... I don't know. Never *acknowledged* what we did and that it was probably a mistake that shouldn't ever happen again."

"I didn't really think it was a mistake." He shrugged. "It was fun. I had a good time, didn't you?"

"Yes, of course I did," she said, with a flush coming to her cheeks as she looked away from his gaze and focused on her place setting instead. "I meant that it probably shouldn't have happened, considering what's going on with your brother and me. Or what I hope to happen once he gets back."

Sawyer wanted to tell Kat not to hold her breath where Finn was concerned, but he wasn't sure if that was being helpful or being bitter. If she wanted to try things with Finn, she'd find out soon enough without him telling her.

"It might not have been the smartest thing I

ever did, but I don't regret it, Kat. It was what it was. And if it never happens again, that's fine." Even as he said the words he knew they weren't really true, but it was what she needed to hear to feel better, so he'd say them.

Kat's gaze met his again. She studied his face, trying to see into his thoughts or something. She would fail. He wasn't even sure how he felt about all this. He understood her concerns about what was developing between them, even as he fought his own urges to spend as much time with her as he could.

"No one ever needs to know about it," he added. "If you and Finn end up one big, happy family, then great for the two of you. I'm not going to stand up and object at the wedding, if that's what you're thinking."

Now it was Kat who looked a little put out. Perhaps he'd been too aloof about their encounter, but he wasn't sure what else to say. Was she expecting him to slam his fist on the table and demand they be together? For him to tell her all the reasons why he was the better choice? What good would that do? She seemed to want his brother even though they both knew Finn wasn't the ideal candidate for dad and husband.

"Oh, okay," she said after a moment. "Well,

then, I guess we just need to put it behind us and there isn't anything more to say about it."

"Very well."

"Speaking of Finn, I heard from him yesterday."

"Oh, really?" Sawyer hadn't spoken to his brother in a while. Finn had been lying low since the news about Kat and the baby had hit the family gossip circuit.

"He says he's coming home next week."

That was news to him. Sawyer had thought he had another couple weeks at least before Finn came back from Beijing. Ideally, he wanted to spend those weeks with Kat in his bed, but since that wasn't going to happen, he supposed it didn't matter when Finn returned.

"That's good to hear," he said, trying not to betray how he really felt. "That means things went well at the new Steele manufacturing facility. There was a bonus for him to open ahead of schedule, as I recall. That should be good for you."

"Why? I don't want any of Finn's money."

"You say that, I know, but you'll end up with something. A trust fund for your daughter, at least?"

Kat reached out anxiously for a corn fritter. "I suppose. He didn't mention anything about work when we spoke. Just that he would be back by next Wednesday afternoon."

"I'm glad to hear it. Then he can be the one here with you instead of me, and I can get back to work. The District closes down in two weeks and I'm going to be up to my neck in blueprints and contractors, getting that place remodeled in my proposed time line. I want it reopened and bustling by the Christmas shopping season. Things went so well in China, maybe I should have Finn handle it," he laughed.

Kat straightened in her seat at the mention of the District, as he'd anticipated. "Yes, I've taken some things home, but I've still got to get all my heavy equipment out. I'll have to hire someone, I suppose, but I've been procrastinating about moving. I guess I was hoping..." Her voice trailed off and she looked at him with her big, optimistic eyes.

"Hoping what? That you'd manage to change my mind and not have to leave?"

They hadn't really lit on this topic since that day at her studio. Other topics, like the baby and getting naked, had taken priority. Sawyer had hoped his argument had been convincing enough to silence her protests, but apparently neither of them had backed down. They'd just been distracted. If Kat was going to give him the cold shoulder and they weren't going to have sex anymore, they might as well return to arguing. That added a little excitement to his day, if nothing else.

"Well, yes," she admitted.

Maybe he had been distracted, but it was possible Kat had been working her side of the argument the whole time. "Is that why you slept with me?" he asked.

The red flush returned to her cheeks. "I would appreciate it if you would stop accusing me of sleeping with you for favors. I told you that wasn't true the first time, after my encounter with Finn, and the answer is the same now. I have not, nor would I ever, use sex as a tool to get my way."

"And yet you admit that you were hoping I would change my mind after the time we've spent together. Was it your stunning argument that you expected to sway me, or did you think you could take advantage of our closeness to get me to change my mind? Tell the truth."

Kat's jaw flexed tightly as she considered her words. "I had hoped that once you got to know me, you would understand where I was coming from. Or that you would be more interested in the plight of the people you're putting out on the street."

"I'm not putting them out on the street. They don't live there. And stop trying to turn me into the bad guy, when you very well could've been manipulating me this whole time."

"Yes, I'm so devious, spending all my time trying to seduce my way through the Steele family!

And even if I did sleep with you to save the District, would it have even worked?"

Sawyer sat back in his chair. If he was honest with himself, she *had* worn away at his defenses. He had listened to her argument. Sunday morning as he'd lain in Kat's bed, he'd considered making changes to his plans just because he thought it might make her smile. But with Finn coming home, there was no sense in admitting that. Perhaps it was better to put an end to whatever was building between them, once and for all. Kat was trying to be polite about distancing herself, but he knew that rarely worked. Anger was like a wrecking ball to anything they'd built.

"Probably not," he said. "Like I told you, it was fun. But sex is sex, and business is business. I never mix the two. It doesn't matter what happened between us or how one of us might feel about the other. The District closes in two weeks for renovations. No reasoned argument or even a heartfelt declaration of love would change that."

Kat looked at him for a moment and then nodded stoically. "I see." She wadded up the cloth napkin in her lap and tossed it onto the table. "I think I'm going to go."

"We haven't eaten yet."

"The baby and I have lost our appetite." Kat scooped up her purse and got to her feet, then brushed past the confused waiter, who held their food in his hands.

They both watched her dart out the door. Sawyer wasn't surprised. He'd said what he'd said on purpose. Her leaving was the inevitable result, as much as it pained him to see her go. Better now than to go through this while he had to watch her with Finn.

"I'll take the burger," he said to the confused man standing with a plate in each hand. "Box up the salad to go. I'll have it for dinner."

Besides, he thought, knowing Kat, this argument was far from over.

"Nice Lexus."

Kat looked up from the box of tools she was packing up and saw Hilda in the doorway. "Hey there."

"I can't help but notice that your attempts to save the District seem to be backfiring spectacularly. Hot sex, billionaire babies, luxury cars, and yet we're still closing in a few weeks."

If those words had come from anyone else, Kat would've been insulted. But she knew Hilda better than that. "I've screwed it all up," she admitted. "Now every time I try to talk to Sawyer, there's family around who want to chat with me and discuss the baby. Pinning him down on the subject is impossible."

"Well, maybe the protest will make a difference. A little negative news coverage for the Steele family might be just what we need to get Sawyer's attention and keep it."

Protest? Oh, no.

Kat dropped her face into her hand. She'd completely forgotten about the protest *she* had organized outside the Steele corporate offices on July Fourth. It was intended to be the artists' way of reclaiming their independence from the new owner. She'd planned it weeks ago as a last-ditch effort to keep the place open if all her other plans failed. Before the wedding. Before she knew about the baby. Before Sawyer was in her bed.

And well before she'd agreed to go out with the same Steele family to celebrate July Fourth on their yacht.

"You forgot, didn't you?"

Kat turned around to face her dearest friend and shook her head in dismay. "How could I have forgotten? I planned the whole thing."

Hilda wrapped her arm around Kat's shoulder. "You haven't missed it yet. No worries. You've had a lot on your plate, hon. You've got pregnancy brain, so do what I do and put everything in your cell phone. If it isn't in my calendar it isn't happening."

"Right. My phone."

Hilda gave her a squeeze and stepped away. "What is it?"

"I… They've invited me to spend the holiday with them."

The older woman looked at her for a moment and then nodded. "Well, you should go."

"I can't! I'm supposed to be the one fighting to save this place. I can't go out on their yacht while I know you guys are out there sweating to death with picket signs and bullhorns. I would feel so hypocritical. I can't. I just can't."

"You're not the only one fighting for the District. You've been our most vocal member, but there are plenty of others here that need to do their part, too. Let them paint their picket signs and march their afternoon away. Maybe it's even better if you aren't there for that. It could cause you some unnecessary angst with your family."

"But *you're* my family. You're all I've got. All that matters."

"Not anymore. You've got new family now. And they're excited to include you in their lives. That's great. I'm very happy for you. It's what you've always wanted."

"But I don't want a new family. I want you and Zeke and everyone else."

Hilda wrapped her in a supportive hug. It was exactly what she needed in that moment, but it wasn't enough to stop the tears from overflowing down her cheeks and wetting her friend's T-shirt.

"We're not going anywhere, Kitty Kat. Family can change, but they never really go away. Whether we're here at the District, or it closes and we scatter to the winds, you'll always be able to find us when you need us. I promise."

It was just like Hilda to say that and refuse to let her feel guilty. "You'll always be there for me, but I'm not going to be there for all of you. I ruined everything. I've lost focus."

"You did nothing of the sort. You've put your focus and your priorities where they belong—on your daughter. Tomorrow, you are going to put on a nice dress and a ton of sunscreen and go enjoy the holiday with your new family. We will carry the torch and things will be just fine. No matter what happens."

Kat opened her mouth to argue, but Hilda held up a finger to silence her. "No matter what happens."

Kat took a deep breath and made herself get out of the Lexus at the marina. There still hadn't been

any word on her Jeep, which made her think that
Sawyer was just humoring her and had no intention of taking back the Lexus. Of course, after the
way their lunch had ended the other day, she might
step outside some morning and find the Lexus
had been towed off to the Steele compound out
of pure spite.

Still, for now she had it, and it was allowing
her to get around town, which she needed to do. If
Finn's attorneys forced some kind of cash settlement on her, the first thing she'd do was pay Sawyer back for the car. She didn't want to feel like
she owed him anything, especially after the ugly
things he'd said.

She'd just been trying to get a little space to
breathe and to think. It was necessary, especially
after that moment they'd shared in the doctor's office. Sitting there, holding his hand and looking at
the baby together had felt special. It felt right in a
way that it shouldn't have. She didn't need those
kinds of thoughts and feelings clouding the situation with Finn. Sawyer had reacted with anger,
only proving that she was correct. They'd gotten
too close and it could jeopardize everything.

Kat hadn't seen or heard from Sawyer since
she'd left the restaurant and that was okay with
her. She'd even planned on sitting out the holiday invitation in favor of protesting with her fel-

low artists, but Jade had called her and insisted she come. Morgan and her husband, River, were back from their honeymoon and wanted to meet her. No excuse seemed to stick with Jade, so now Kat was about to spend several hours on a small boat with Sawyer and his family in the middle of the harbor. Space was not an option.

She eyed the boats docked at the marina and her gaze caught the name of the biggest one: *License to Drill*. No doubt that belonged to the tool magnate Steele family. It looked like it had to be nearly two hundred feet in length, towering over the other boats, with four decks reaching to the sky. Maybe she would be able to avoid Sawyer after all.

As she headed that way, she noticed two women standing on the lowest deck. They were like day and night, blond and brunette. As she got closer, she recognized the blonde as Jade. That meant there would be at least one smiling face there to welcome her today and counteract Sawyer's grumpy countenance.

"Kat! You made it!" Jade was looking her direction and waving.

She waved back and walked up the pier to the stairs, where she could come aboard. The two women were there to meet her. "Kat, this is Morgan. She's finally back from her honeymoon."

"Hey, my first honeymoon was such a mess,

we decided this one was going to be extra special. I highly recommend Fiji." The dark-haired woman with the golden tan smiled and stuck out her hand. "I'm Morgan Atkinson. I'm still getting used to saying that."

"I'm Kat," she responded, shaking her hand. "I'm sorry if I caused a problem at your wedding."

Morgan waved away her concerns. "It's not a problem. I'm only sad I missed you slapping the daylights out of Sawyer. I know Finn is the one who deserved it, but Sawyer can be a smug little jerk when he wants to be, too."

"Come on," Jade said. "Let's get you settled in and introduced to everyone. I think you're the last to arrive, so we should be departing soon. Morgan's husband, River, is here, and my fiancé, Harley, is around somewhere. Probably hiding from my parents. And Grandma is here, of course. She's excited to get to spend more time with you. We're hoping this time she shares. No one was able to get a word in with you or her at the party Saturday."

"What about Sawyer?" Kat asked, as they climbed a set of stairs to a higher deck.

"He's here. He was chatting up River about construction last I saw them."

That didn't surprise Kat. He probably had drywall and electrical conduits on his brain, with less than two weeks to closing the District.

The women led her through the luxurious interior of the yacht to the elevator. Looking around, Kat had a hard time believing she wasn't in a hotel. There was art on the walls, marble on the floors and polished wood everywhere. Everything was shiny and expensive, with inlaid gold, onyx and mother of pearl, making her feel incredibly out of place and wondering if she still had sawdust in her hair from working at the studio that morning.

They stepped out of the elevator onto one of the higher decks, where the rest of the family was gathered under shade sails around a hot tub and lounging area. Everyone cheered as she made her entrance, and the girls introduced her to the people she hadn't met yet. They mingled and nibbled on canapés while sipping cocktails and enjoying the sea breeze. Kat chose her seltzer and a seat far from Sawyer where she could protect her fair skin from the sun.

The rest of the afternoon was a blur. Once they set sail, the family moved inside, to where a "casual" buffet dinner of shrimp kabobs, baby back ribs, fire-roasted corn and twice-baked potatoes had been set up for them. The family seemed much more at ease without a bunch of guests around. They laughed, sipped their drinks, told Kat embarrassing stories about Finn and pumped her for information about the baby. When she finally told them it was a girl, there were more cheers of excitement.

After a few hours, Kat found herself really enjoying this time with the Steeles. She was having more fun with them than she'd ever expected to. They were remarkably down to earth once you set aside the luxurious surroundings. After eating, some people played cards on the top deck, while others went to a lower lounge to watch the water from shaded sofas. Kat was included in every conversation and game. They didn't look at her with suspicion the way she'd thought they might, nor did anyone pin her in a corner to grill her. Aside from Sawyer generally avoiding her, everyone was friendly and welcoming. Just the way she imagined a family was supposed to be.

She had no idea how things were going to go with Finn when he returned. She had her fingers crossed about that. But if she liked him half as much as she did the rest of this family, they might have a chance. Kat hadn't intended to start a family this way, but it seemed as if her daughter would at least get some decent aunts and uncles out of it.

"You guys need to come outside to the top deck if you're going to watch the fireworks the city is setting off over the harbor. We've got a surprise, too," Morgan said.

Kat had been watching Sawyer and Harley battle each other at chess when they heard the call from above. She was surprised to notice the sun had gone down while they were playing. When she reached the top deck, she noticed the whole boat was lit with pink light.

"Surprise!" Jade and Morgan said, as she stepped out.

"How did you turn the yacht pink?" she asked in amazement.

"All the lights are remote controlled fluorescents and can change to over two hundred thousand color combinations. Tonight, in honor of Baby Girl Steele, it's going to be pink. I don't care if it's the Fourth of July," Morgan declared.

"We've got a few minutes before the fireworks start," Jade said. "Come with us to get some drinks."

Kat followed the girls to the bar, where a gentleman in a polo shirt embroidered with the name of the yacht was waiting to make them a drink. She took her club soda and cranberry juice back with her, enjoying the view from the deck now that the sun had set. Charleston lit up, with the bridge stretching across the waterway and the Yorktown in the distance, was a stunning sight.

The three of them settled in a private area of clustered couches, away from the rest of the crowd on the third deck.

"Okay, so without everyone else around to hear, I'm curious about what's going on with you and Finn," Jade pressed.

Kat placed her drink on the table and settled back in her seat. "Not much, yet. But I'm hopeful for more than what his lawyers offered."

"Was he being cheap?" Morgan asked, an appalled look on her face.

"No, not at all. He was extremely generous, actually. But I guess I'm looking for something different from him. To be honest, what I want is a family for my child. For us both. I grew up with busy parents who were always working, and then they were gone and I was all alone in the world. I want to do this differently. I don't just want money from Finn, I want his time. Real, quality time."

"Do you want to get married?" Jade asked. "It seems like a big leap after a single date, especially for Finn, but I'm sure that's what Dad is going to be pushing for."

"Yes," Kat admitted. "I know it seems silly in this day and age, but I do want to get married to my baby's father. I know I don't love Finn and he doesn't love me, but this is about more than that. It's about creating a supportive and loving environment for the baby to grow up in. Maybe love will come in time. I don't know. I can only hope that Finn will step up and do the right thing, and that everything works out."

"Well, Finn is always surprising people," Morgan said. "I hope for your sake that he takes this seriously and you get everything you're hoping for. Then you can name the baby after her sweet and supportive Aunt Morgan."

Nine

Sawyer didn't pay much attention to the fireworks, the patriotic music or the impressive desserts the yacht's chef brought out when they were over. No, his mind was someplace else, thanks to overhearing Kat's discussion with his sisters.

After she'd walked out on him at lunch the other day, he couldn't decide if he was irritated or grateful. She'd pushed him away and he'd pushed back twice as hard on reflex. Maybe it was for the best, after everything he'd overheard tonight, but he couldn't help but feel like crap since it happened. He wanted to apologize for the ugly things he'd said. He'd almost pulled her aside twice today to do just that. The first time he'd been stopped by a text from Steele security about District protesters outside their corporate offices. Even with Kat on the boat with him, he knew she was behind it. He'd stewed about it for a while and then went to find her again after his chess game. He found her with his sisters and hesitated. Now that he'd heard what she'd said to Jade and Morgan, he was glad he hadn't spoken to her alone. He needed to butt out of the whole situation.

Kat wanted to marry Finn and live happily ever after with their daughter. She knew the odds were stacked against her, and yet she wanted the best for her baby, and he could tell she wouldn't rest until she had it. Before Finn even knew what hit him, he'd be swept away in a tide of domesticity. He'd own a nice house in a good school district, drive a minivan and be celebrating his fifth wedding anniversary with Kat. Somehow, he did everything wrong and was going to be rewarded with a woman and a life he didn't deserve.

For the third time in recent memory, Sawyer was practically green with jealously of Finn. He hated that feeling.

And so he'd started smothering it with alcohol. Or trying to. The Scotch had unfortunately kicked in right about the time the yacht returned to port and everyone was unloading to go home.

Sawyer ordered a coffee and chugged it so hot he burned his tongue, but he wasn't sure it was going to be enough. He stumbled a bit heading down the stairs, but was lucky enough for Harley to be there and keep him from hitting the deck with his face.

"Whoa, there. Do we need to call you a car, Sawyer?" Harley asked. "I'd give you a ride, but you live the wrong way."

"Shh," Sawyer slurred, and looked around for Trevor and Patricia. "Don't make a fuss about it or my folks will make me ride home with them and stay at the house. I do not want to sober up with our housekeeper's homemade hangover juice."

"Ugh," Morgan groaned. "I think Lena just made us drink that as a punishment for partying as teenagers. It doesn't help the hangover at all."

"Well, you can't drive. Can you just sleep over on the boat tonight?"

"I'll take him home. I'm pretty sure it's on my way. Pregnant women are nature's designated drivers, anyway."

Sawyer turned around to see Kat standing nearby. She was the last person he needed to be alone with while his filter was down and his tongue was loose. "You don't have to do that. I'll talk to the captain about crashing here."

"No, you won't. You drove me home when my Jeep wouldn't start. I owe you one. Just promise me you won't throw up in the Lexus. You can't re-gift a car that smells like puke."

She smiled at her joke and his heart started racing in his chest. Kat had a light sweater pulled over her bare shoulders to protect from the chill of the sea air, but earlier, she'd worn only the strapless navy blue sundress. Her hair was pulled back into a high ponytail and it swung back and forth when she walked. He'd wanted to tell her how beautiful she looked today, casual and elegant, but it had seemed like a bad idea. Lately, all his ideas were bad ones.

"I promise," he said instead. Perhaps some time alone would be what he needed to apologize, and then both of them could move on.

Harley and River helped Sawyer walk off the boat, and loaded him into her passenger seat while Morgan put Sawyer's address into the GPS. "Are you sure you can handle him?" Harley asked with concerned eyes.

Kat nodded and climbed into the car beside him. "I'll be fine. I'll just slap him when we get to his place and he'll wake right up."

Harley's and River's laughter was muted by the

slamming of the car door. As she started the engine, Sawyer pushed himself up in the seat and put on his seat belt for the ride.

"Thank you for driving me home even though you hate me."

"It's not a problem, and I don't hate you. You might be a jerk sometimes, but I don't want you driving if it isn't safe."

"I'm sorry," he said, after an extended silence.

Kat turned to him for a moment before merging into the traffic and heading to his place. "You're sorry for what?"

"For everything I said to you the other day. I was upset when you said we were over, and I lashed out at you. That wasn't the right thing to do. I know now that you just want what's best for your daughter and that's to be with her father. I shouldn't be angry or try to stand in the way of that. I only want what's best for you and the baby, too."

She seemed stunned by his apology, letting the words sink in before she finally responded. "Thank you, Sawyer. I'm sorry, too. I guess we both could've handled it better. I never should've entertained something with you when I knew what I wanted with Finn. I should've told you."

With the air clear, they drove in silence across the peninsula until they closed in on his place.

"You have reached your destination," the GPS announced, disrupting the quiet inside the car as she pulled up in front of his house.

"You can turn into the drive just there." Sawyer pointed and hit a button on his key chain to open the gate to his private driveway.

She turned in and came to a stop, shutting off the engine. "Let's get you inside."

Sawyer looked at her with confusion. "You're coming in?"

Her pointed expression shot down any thoughts he might entertain about her inside his house. "I'm going to help you up the stairs and get you in the house. If you behave, I might make you some coffee and toast."

Sawyer nodded and opened the car door. He was feeling pretty steady on his feet now, but as they moved toward the stairs, he felt less sure. Kat was quick to move to his side. She wrapped his arm around her shoulders and put hers around his waist.

"Grab the rail and help me," she said, so he did.

It took three times fumbling with his keys and dropping them, but they finally made it inside his place. He stumbled in, shrugging out of his blazer and tossing it onto a wingback chair like he did every night. His keys went into a bowl by the door as he flipped on the overhead light.

He paused as Kat gasped, and figured the original rose medallion in the ceiling, along with the restored crystal chandelier, had caught her eye. Instead, when he turned, she was running her hand over the ornately carved wood of the staircase just to their right.

"The woodwork is beautiful."

Sawyer looked around his living room and nodded. "I forget you're a wood carver. You'll find a lot you'll like here. Much of the house had already been redone when I bought it, but thankfully, they left most of the original woodwork intact. The decorator I hired did a good job incorporating the existing historical details into my modern aesthetic."

"I'm surprised you got all those words past your tongue," Kat said with a smile.

"Very funny. The kitchen is this way."

Kat followed him through the living room and into the kitchen at the rear of the house. He'd had it done in all white, with black hardware and dark antique fixtures for a stark, clean look. It seemed to go well with the original white shiplap that ran through the home and the tiny white octagon tiles on the floor.

She strolled through the kitchen, touching the quartz countertop and the faucet before bending over to look at the wood cabinetry of the island. He'd had that piece done by a local carpenter who carved the details by hand. Kat noticed immediately, running her fingers over the scrollwork.

"You don't even cook in here, do you?" she asked, as she stood back up.

He shook his head, making himself dizzy, so he sat on a bar stool on the other side of the kitchen island. "I like things with clean lines, and designs that look tidy. I also like features that will help with resale down the road. This seemed like a good mix, whether I use it or not. And I have used the microwave," he said, pointing out the stainless-steel machine mounted into the side of the island. "And the coffee maker."

Kat nodded thoughtfully. "Well, speaking of coffee makers, you have been a good boy so far. I believe I promised you coffee and toast."

"Coffee is in that jar, and bread is in the pantry over there."

She followed his guidance, moving around the kitchen to prepare a late-night drunk man's snack. A few minutes later, she presented him with a steaming mug of black coffee and a plate with two dry pieces of toast on it.

"It's not haute cuisine, but it's what you need. When you're done, we'll follow it up with a big glass of water and some ibuprofen. You'll wake up feeling like a champ."

"You know a lot about being drunk."

Kat shrugged. "I went to college, same as you. Late-night parties followed by early morning lectures mean you learn how to cope, and quickly. I also lost my parents when I was in school. There are a few weekends I don't remember after that happened. Water, Advil, toast and coffee are a combination that never fails."

"I think I would've failed the semester if I lost my parents."

"Well, fortunately, I went to an art school. They encouraged me to funnel my pain into my work, and my grades actually improved. Except for chemistry. I got a D in that," she said with a smile.

Sawyer chuckled and finished his requisite meal quickly. As she put his dishes into the sink, he went over to the refrigerator and pulled out two bottles of water. "Here you go," he said, handing her one.

"Thanks. How are you feeling?"

"Better. It all seemed to hit at once tonight. Drinking that late was foolish," he admitted. "But it got you here. I can't complain about that."

Kat set her water on the counter and looked at him with amusement crinkling her eyes. "Did you set all this up to get me to your house?"

"No," he said, with a dismissive shake of his head. "Lately nothing I plan works out as well as I want it to, so I've decided to give that up. Sometimes it's better to just go with the flow and see what happens. It always works for Finn, so why not me?"

She narrowed her gaze at him. "You're not Finn. You're Sawyer."

He shrugged and finished off his water. "Fat lot of good that does me. Finn is the one who reaps all the rewards. He has all the fun, gets all the girls, lives life to the fullest. He always gets what I want," Sawyer said, looking pointedly at Kat.

She dismissed his inebriated tirade, stretching out her hand and gently grasping his wrist. "You may look alike, but the world needs only one Finn. And it needs you to be yourself, because there's only one you."

Sawyer looked down at her hand and followed the line of her arm until he was gazing into her eyes. "Stay with me tonight."

Kat froze for a moment before dropping her hand from his wrist. He could tell by the line between her brows that she was conflicted. She wanted to stay. She wanted him. But she kept putting this fantasy of a future with Finn in front of her own needs and desires.

"Just one night. One last time."

She backed up until she hit the quartz countertop of the island. "You've been drinking. You don't mean it. We both agreed it was a mistake the last time."

He took a step forward and shook his head. "I know exactly what I'm saying, Kat. I'm not that drunk."

"I don't know, Sawyer. I—"

He took another step, but she didn't move away. "Finn will be home soon. And if you get what you want, everything that happened between us will be a deeply buried secret once you move on with your life. I will become your brother-in-law or the baby's uncle Sawyer. Nothing more. And I'll be okay with that, because it's what you want. But give me one last night to keep with me. A night to remember you by."

Sawyer reached out to capture the ever-present strand of auburn hair that fell along her cheek, and pushed it behind her ear. He let his knuckles graze her skin and felt her press into his touch.

"Please, Kat."

There was something in his voice. In the way he looked at her. Something that told Kat she wasn't going to be able to walk away from him. Not to-night.

She closed her eyes and leaned into the warm fingers brushing against her face. She longed to have those same warm hands on her body and his lips pressed to hers. These last few days, she'd missed Sawyer. Whether he was aggravating her or making love to her, she missed it. And she knew she would miss it for the days and weeks to come.

Why not indulge one last time? Give them both something to remember?

Opening her eyes, she closed the gap between them, cradled his face in her hands and pulled his mouth to hers. The rough stubble of his evening beard prickled against her hands in sharp contrast to her own soft skin.

The moment he realized she wasn't just kissing him, but saying yes to his proposition, the intensity increased tenfold. His arms wrapped around her, pulling her tight against him with the hunger of a man who'd long denied himself sustenance. He pressed her back against the island, his hands roaming across her body just as his tongue explored her mouth.

Kat met his intensity. With everything she had, she wanted him. And if it was the last time, she wanted to remember every moment in his arms.

Her breathing quickened when his lips traveled along her jaw and down her throat. He licked and nibbled at her skin, causing Kat to gasp and writhe as the pleasurable tingles vibrated through her nervous system. Her neck was her weakness and Sawyer instinctively seemed to know it. As her knees softened beneath her from the sensations, he tightened his grip, holding her upright.

And then, when she needed him more than ever, he retreated. She opened her eyes to see him looking down at her with desire blazing in his dark gaze. He seemed pensive, and it scared her. He wasn't changing his mind, was he? Then he took a step back, helping her regain her footing, and reached for her hand. "Come on."

"Where are we going?" she asked.

"I'm taking you upstairs," he said. "If this is the last time we'll be together, I'm going to do it properly, not some quick tumble on the closest hard surface."

She followed him back to the staircase she'd admired earlier, and they went up to the second floor. There, he opened a pair of French doors to the master suite, which took up the majority of that level. In the center of the room was the show-piece—a grand four-poster bed that was carved to look like ivy was wrapped around its massive columns and across the headboard.

Kat couldn't stop herself from walking up to it and touching one of the columns. It was an old piece. Better than her own work, she had to admit. It was beautiful. Perhaps the most beautiful bed she'd ever seen. She had the sudden burning urge to go to her shop and make a headboard at her first opportunity.

"I found this in the attic when I bought the house," Sawyer said, as he came up behind her and ran his own hand over the smooth, polished wood. "I had it restored and refinished. I must've known you would be here to see it one day."

Kat turned to face him, looking up at the dark eyes that watched her so carefully. He reached out to brush the hair from her face again and then softly ran his thumb over her bottom lip. Even as he teetered on the edge of being tipsy, he was more thoughtful and loving than any man she'd ever been with.

His attention to detail continued as they moved around to the side of the bed. They slowly removed each other's clothing, caressing and kissing the bare skin as they exposed it. Then he picked her up around the waist and lifted her onto the high mattress. She scooted back as he advanced, covering her body with his until his warm skin chased away the cool conditioned air being circulated by the ceiling fan overhead.

Sawyer propped himself on his elbows, looking down at her. Kat wished she knew what he was thinking, but she was too afraid to ask. Knowing the truth would only make things harder.

He slipped between her thighs, rubbing his

hands over the outside of her legs and hips until she nearly purred from the caress. He dipped his head, drawing one of her nipples into his mouth. Sawyer teased it, tugging hard on her flesh until her back arched up off the bed.

Kat dug her heels into the mattress, lifting her hips and seeking him out. He didn't disappoint, moving forward into her without much effort. She was ready for him, welcoming him inside with a hiss of satisfaction.

From there, he took his time. He wanted a night to remember and they would have it. Every inch of her skin was caressed and kissed. Every sound she made he seemed to memorize. When he moved inside her with more urgency, Kat fought to keep her eyes open so she, too, could remember every moment.

Eventually, she lost that battle. Her release exploded inside her just as his mouth clamped down onto hers. He swallowed her cries, taking them into himself for safekeeping and mingling them with his own low groans as he poured himself into her.

It was a leisurely, but emotionally exhausting, lovemaking session. And when Sawyer collapsed at her side, he was curled up next to her with his hand protectively resting on her belly.

Kat knew it then. If she was being honest with

herself, she'd known it before. She'd known it the first night they spent together, but she'd been too stubborn to believe it. It wasn't a part of her plan. It wasn't the way she wanted things to turn out. But that didn't make it any less true.

Kat was in love with Sawyer.

She could tell herself that she wanted to marry Finn, but that was just her own head getting in the way of what her heart wanted. She hardly knew Finn. But what she did know was that there was no way he could compete with Sawyer. His twin had already taken his place in her heart and no matter how hard she tried to push him out, Sawyer was still there.

She closed her eyes tightly and cursed herself. She was an idiot. She'd gone and fallen in love with the wrong Steele twin.

Turning her head, she looked over at him. His eyes were closed, his golden lashes resting on his cheeks. He'd already fallen fast asleep, thanks to the combined sedative effects of good sex and strong whiskey. She wanted to tell him how she felt, but seeing him asleep was enough to give her pause.

Sawyer was a good man. He was as stubborn as she was, for sure, but he had a very strong compass when it came to right and wrong. That he'd given in to his desire for her, even knowing it wasn't right, had to mean something. It meant he cared for her, too, no matter if he knew or understood that himself.

But that moral compass wasn't going anywhere. He'd asked her for one last night and that's all he would take. Once Finn was back in Charleston, he would step aside just as he'd said he would. Even if it hurt him. Even if it broke his heart to do it. And telling him that she loved him wouldn't help. It would only make it harder on both of them. She knew he would put the baby's needs first, just like she had.

And nothing short of a time machine would change the fact that Finn was her baby's father.

Ten

"*Nǐ hǎo. Wǒ huíláile!*"

Sawyer looked up from his computer and inwardly cringed at the sound of his brother's voice and his massacred attempt at speaking Mandarin as he came down the hallway.

Finn stopped in Sawyer's doorway. He was wearing his usual suit, but instead of a tie, his shirt collar was unbuttoned to show a gold necklace with a jade medallion he'd picked up overseas. "I have returned, twin of mine. Did you miss me?"

"Not particularly," Sawyer said flatly.

Finn smiled and continued down the hall without missing a beat. Sawyer didn't really want to follow, but he wanted to know how things had gone in China, and his father would probably be demanding a full report immediately.

Pushing up from his chair, he went out and followed Finn to the big corner office where Trevor Steele held court. His brother was already in there by the time he reached the assistant's desk.

"Sawyer, come in and shut the door," Trevor said.

Finn was grinning from ear to ear in one of the two guest chairs across from their father. Things must have gone well in Beijing. Or his brother was too busy doing other things to notice that it hadn't.

"The manufacturing plant is complete and operational. I returned home for a few weeks while the staffing team works on hiring from the local area and getting the team trained. I think we will have them punching out hammers and sockets within a month, conservatively."

Both brothers turned to Trevor for his reaction and Sawyer wasn't disappointed.

"Thanks for the update," Trevor retorted, "but I know exactly what's going on over there. Do you really think I'd send you halfway across the world to manage a multi-million-dollar operation and not know what was going on every second of the day?"

Finn's smile faded. "Of course you would keep

abreast. You're the president of the company. I just wanted to share the good news with you and Sawyer."

Trevor sat back in his chair and crossed his hands over his chest. "You did fine, son. Better than I expected, really. But it's hard for me to focus on that considering the mess you left behind at home."

"Mess?"

Sawyer's hands curled into fists on the arms of his chair. Completely oblivious as usual. "He's talking about Kat and the baby, you idiot."

"That's not a mess," Finn argued, looking between his father and his brother. "My attorneys have it all handled. I'm going to meet with her this week to negotiate a settlement and get her to sign off. It's fine."

Trevor studied his sons for a moment and then pinched the bridge of his nose. "I don't know how the two of you could look so similar and be so different. You are a damn fool, Finn. It's not fine. You got a stranger pregnant."

"It was an accident! I assure you I did, and always have done, everything in my power to keep that from happening."

"Everything short of keeping it in your pants," Trevor snapped.

While Sawyer did enjoy Finn getting his come-uppance on some level, he was growing uncomfortable being in the room. "Do I really need to be in here for this? I thought we were out-briefing on the new facility."

He started to push up from his chair, but Trevor's sharp gaze caused him to sit back down immediately. "You stay," he said. "You've been the one handling things with Kat while he's been gone. You know her better than anyone."

"I don't see what the problem is," Finn argued. "I plan to take care of Kat and the baby."

"That's not enough. Writing a check and walking away from your responsibilities is not enough. You've forgotten that I've met this woman. Your mother met her. Your grandmother and sisters have met her. And they like her. *I* like her. She's not your usual weekend delight that you can give a check to and send on her way. She's more your brother's speed, to be honest, but she had the misfortune of meeting the wrong Steele twin. She is smart and kind, and the best damn thing to ever happen to you. She could be the thing that turns your life around. And accident or no accident, she deserves better than what you're offering."

"You don't even know what I'm offering."

"I know what you're *not* offering," their father said sharply. "You know, I sent you to China in the hopes you would grow up. You're almost thirty-four years old and you've been causing problems for the family since you found that pecker between your legs. Now it looks like I'm going to have to make you man up once and for all."

Finn was pressed back so far in his chair, Sawyer thought he might tumble backward. He was smart enough not to say anything else at this point. Even Finn knew when to shut up and just listen.

"That is your child, and you're going to marry its mother. Steeles don't walk away from their mistakes."

"Only when we can't erase them and pretend like they never happened," Finn said.

Sawyer's eyes widened as he looked at his brother in shock. Maybe Finn wasn't as smart as he thought.

"What did you say?" Trevor asked in a biting, sarcastic tone.

"I'm talking about Morgan and how your *guiding hand* completely destroyed her life. You paid off River and just swept her marriage and her baby under the rug, but you can't do that with me, so you're bullying me into doing what you want instead."

Sawyer was afraid to take a breath. He sat still, waiting for the blowback. He'd never heard Finn— or anyone for that matter—speak to their father that way. He could see the anger twitching the muscles in his father's jaw as he considered his words.

"You're right," Trevor said at last, in a cold, calm voice. "I thought at nineteen that Morgan was too young and immature to make her own decisions and I was wrong. But this time, I'm right, and you've just proved you're still too immature to make your own decisions."

Finn didn't have anything to say to that. Neither did Sawyer. What could he say? This was what Kat wanted, although she probably would've preferred it not be a shotgun wedding.

"Tomorrow night, we'll have a nice family dinner to welcome you home. We will invite Kat. And there, in front of everyone, you're going to present her with an engagement ring and ask her to be your wife. Do you understand me?"

Finn swallowed hard and nodded.

"Very good. Now give your travel paperwork and receipts to your assistant to file and go get some rest. You're dismissed." Both brothers stood up, but Trevor's gaze shot to Sawyer. "Not you."

Finn basically ran from the office, leaving Sawyer behind. He sighed and sat back in the chair, awaiting whatever tongue-lashing he'd earned lately. His father probably knew about him sneaking around with Kat. The man seemed to know everything that happened in this family.

"What am I going to do with him?" Trevor asked with a heavy sigh.

"If you make him marry her, he's going to be miserable. And he'll make everyone else miserable, including Kat."

"I know. But at some point, he needs to take responsibility."

"Let me marry her instead." The words slipped from Sawyer's lips before he'd fully thought them through. He didn't regret them, though.

Trevor snapped his gaze over to his son. "That's a generous offer. Would you care to tell me why you'd like to marry Kat in your brother's place?"

"It's the best solution," Sawyer argued. "Finn doesn't want to do it, but I will, and the problem will be solved. Genetically, legally, it will be my child as much as Finn's. She will look just like me. No one ever needs to know the truth."

His father considered his words for a moment and shook his head. "That's very pragmatic of you. I can always count on you to do what needs to be done, although I'm sure in this case there's more to your motivations than I really want to know. But I can't let you do that."

"Why not?"

"Because this isn't about you. If you want to help, then I need you to back off and let Finn step up. Let things play out between the two of them. If he proposes and Kat turns him down to choose you instead, let that be *her* choice. If she has any damn sense, she would laugh in his face, but Finn has to make the effort or he never will."

Sawyer sighed. His father was right. This was Kat's decision. They could sit in this office and make all the plans in the world, but in the end, only what she wanted mattered. And as far as Sawyer knew, she wanted Finn. "Is there anything else?"

"Yes. That protest over the holiday. It was all over the news this weekend. That's blowback from your real estate deal, isn't it?"

Sawyer had hoped maybe word hadn't gotten to his father about that yet, but clearly he wasn't that lucky. "Yes."

"It's one thing to try to make money on a property deal, but I'll not have you dragging the family or the company through the mud to do it. Find out a way to make those people happy. Sometimes compromise is key, in business and in romance."

Oddly, this was a little bit of both for Sawyer. But his father was right. There had to be a middle ground that would keep protests off the front pages. The new building could be amazing, but it wouldn't matter if no one was willing to cross a picket line to see it. "Yes, sir."

"One last thing and you can go. Take your brother to the jewelry store. Make sure he picks something nice. Nothing gaudy or cheap. I don't want her turning him down just because he got her the Tuesday cubic zirconia special from Big Eddie on King Street."

Sawyer stood up and nodded. Helping his brother pick out an engagement ring for Kat was one of the last things he wanted to do, but he would to make sure she got something she would love. She deserved that much.

After stepping out into the hall, he headed back toward his office. There, he found Finn sitting on the edge of their assistant's desk, flirting mercilessly as though that wasn't a lawsuit waiting to happen.

"Come on, Finn, we need to go engagement ring shopping so you can propose tomorrow night."

Their assistant, Melody May, sat up at attention and pulled back from Finn. The smile faded from her face and she snatched the travel receipts from his hand without another word.

Finn matched her frown and followed Sawyer into his office. "You really think I should do this? Are you as crazy as Dad?"

"Shut the door," Sawyer said as he leaned against his desk. "And sit down."

"I just got one ass chewing. You don't get to boss me around, too."

"I'm older by two minutes. Now shut the damn door," he barked, pointing to the entrance, "and listen to me."

Finn reluctantly complied and flopped down into the guest chair. "What?"

"A lot has happened while you've been gone. We've all gotten to know Kat very well. Better than you know her. And like Dad said, we like her. The only thing wrong with her is that for some crazy reason, she seems to think that marrying you is the right thing to do. Personally, I think she could do better, but she hasn't asked my opinion."

"What's your point?" Finn said, crossing his arms defiantly over his chest.

Sawyer leaned in to his brother with his stoniest gaze. "My point is that Katherine McIntyre is the single greatest woman to ever walk into your life. She is smart, funny, talented, beautiful…and she's having your child. You don't deserve her in your bed and you don't deserve her as your wife. Not even close. But right now she's there for the taking. And if you let her walk out of your life, you're an even bigger fool than I thought."

"Good evening, Miss McIntyre," Lena said, as she opened the door to the Steele mansion. "Please come in. The family is in the library."

Kat stepped in cautiously and waited for Lena to close the door behind her before she started making her way toward the voices in the east wing of the house.

"Kat!" A woman's voice boomed across the entryway.

She turned to see Morgan rushing over to her from the stairs. "Hey."

Without a word, she grabbed Kat's hand and dragged her away from the library toward the powder room. She tugged her inside and shut the door.

"What is going on?" Kat asked, awkwardly pressed against the pedestal sink.

"Finn is proposing to you at dinner tonight," Morgan blurted in excitement.

Kat's jaw dropped. "Are you serious? I haven't even seen him since he got back from China. We've spoken a handful of times on the phone. Proposing tonight? Really?"

Morgan nodded, a conspiratorial look on her face. "I've seen the ring. Sawyer took him shopping yesterday and it's ah-mazing."

She was stunned. This was just supposed to be a welcome-home dinner with the family. Her chance to see and talk to Finn in person for the first time since the night they'd gotten themselves into this mess. And he was proposing? In the moment, she wasn't sure what to say. Thank goodness Morgan had given her a heads-up or she might've appeared like a very ungrateful recipient when Finn popped the question. After all, this was what she wanted.

Right?

"Anyway, I thought you should know. It ruins the surprise, but personally, I'd rather be prepared. If he does it in front of the whole family, it could be nerve-racking. Plus, I wanted to squeal a little with you about it ahead of time. This is just what you said you wanted the other night on the ship! I'm so happy for you!"

Morgan scooped Kat into a hug and she returned the embrace. Why was her future sister-in-law more excited about this than she was? She pinched her eyes shut and tried to push the image of Sawyer out of her mind. That was over and done. He was stepping aside so Kat could have the family she wanted. It was all coming together.

"Okay, I'd better get back before someone wonders where I've been. See you in there in a minute." Morgan opened the door and dashed out of the bathroom.

Kat took a moment to compose herself. She checked her makeup and smoothed her hair. She wanted to look perfect for the moment. Finn should be proud of his bride, whether he'd intended for this to happen or not. After stepping out of the room, she turned and very nearly collided with Sawyer as he hung his coat in the nearby closet.

"Kat? I didn't know you were here already. Are you hiding in the bathroom?"

"Of course not. I was just putting on some fresh lipstick."

He nodded, trying and failing to look disinterested in her appearance tonight. "Have you seen Finn yet?"

"No. I saw Morgan briefly, but that's it so far."

He nodded again. There was a stiffness about Sawyer tonight. If he took Finn shopping, then he knew what was about to happen. He didn't seem to like the idea very much. Lately, neither did she. It made her want to ask the hard questions while she still had the chance.

"Can I ask you something before we go in there with your family?"

"Sure," he said, pasting on a polite smile.

Kat tried to think of how best to ask the question. "Can you give me any reason why I shouldn't marry Finn?"

She wanted to give him his chance. His moment. Not to do the honorable thing, but to tell the truth about how he felt about her, even if it turned the whole night upside down. Her eyes searched his face, pleading with him to be honest. Marrying Finn had seemed like a good idea until Sawyer showed up in her life. Now, she wasn't sure what she wanted, but knowing if he loved her the way she loved him would help her decide.

"I'm sorry, I can't," he said, looking away. Without making additional eye contact, Sawyer turned and walked across the hall, leaving her there alone and brokenhearted.

The rest of the evening was a bit of a blur, like she was walking through a dream. Kat was distracted and wallowing in her emotional turmoil. They gathered in the library for drinks and mingling before moving into the dining room.

As they migrated down the hall, Finn pulled Kat aside to chat in person at last. It was weird seeing him again after all this time, knowing he was her baby's father, looking so much like the man she loved but not like him at all. Later, as they were eating, she realized she couldn't really remember anything about their conversation. It had mostly been about himself and his work in China. Not once had he asked about her, the pregnancy or the baby. It made the news of his pending return to Beijing in a few weeks a little easier to swallow.

Besides that, it was hard to focus with Sawyer scowling at them. In the library, he'd pretended to be listening to what Grandma Ingrid had to say, but every time Kat glanced in his direction, he'd been looking at her as if he regretted not taking his chance when he had it.

Dinner wasn't much better. She was seated beside Finn, of course, but somehow ended up across from Sawyer. While she tried to engage Finn and

River, to her right, in conversation as they ate, she could feel Sawyer's gaze on her.

She wasn't sure how she was going to get through tonight. When the moment came, and Finn got down on one knee, how could she say yes with Sawyer watching? It seemed the thing she'd once hoped for had become an impossible feat.

As Lena cleared the dinner dishes in preparation for dessert, Finn pushed back his chair to make a toast. Kat froze in her seat, finally forcing herself to reach out and raise her glass of sparkling water.

"I'd like to thank everyone for coming tonight and welcoming me home from China. It was an amazing trip and I look forward to returning and continuing to assist in Steele Tools' new venture there. It's such a fast-paced and colorful culture in some aspects, and then so peaceful and quiet in other areas. I was able to find something for each one of you on my trip. The bag of goodies is in the library and I'll hand them out after dessert. But right now, I have one special gift for Kat. I—"

Sawyer abruptly pushed his chair back from the dinner table. "You'll have to excuse me," he said, as he rounded the long table and practically ran into the hall.

Everyone sat in stunned silence for a moment before Finn recovered. "I hope he's feeling okay. Anyway, I wanted to thank all of you for welcoming Kat so warmly into the family while I was gone. I have heard nothing but glowing stories about what a talented and lovely woman she is. And although we haven't known each other for long, I look forward to having the opportunity to know her very well in the upcoming years."

As Finn reached into his suit coat pocket, Kat's heart started pounding in her chest. For a moment, all she could hear was its deep bass rhythm and the rushing of blood in her ears. She thought she might even faint. She closed her eyes, hoping the swimming in her head would pass before she made a fool of herself in front of these lovely people who had welcomed her into their family.

When she opened her eyes, she realized that Finn was down on his knee beside her. He had a small jewelry box in one hand, opened to display one of the most beautiful rings she'd ever seen in her life. The diamond in the center was a large and colorless oval stone, but what really caught her eye was the platinum band itself. The diamond was in a bezel setting with a knife edge designed band. There were three diamonds on each side that tapered in size to a double milgrain design. She could tell the intricate filigree etching had been hand done by an artisan who loved to work with metal and jewelry design as much as she enjoyed working with wood.

"Katherine McIntyre, I know that we are only at the start of our journey together. Tonight I offer you this ring in the hopes that it will be a long, happy one. Will you marry me?"

She didn't know what to say.

It was the moment she'd been waiting for. This might have started off by accident, but Finn was stepping up and helping her achieve her dream of having a real family for her daughter. Mother, wife, father, husband, child, family…it was all coming together. There was only one thing missing from the picture.

Love.

Kat had told herself she didn't need it. What the baby needed was more important. She'd told herself that if Finn would marry her, she would make a good life with him and maybe love would come in time.

The moment was right. The ring was perfect. The proposal was heartfelt and well-spoken. She was surrounded by her new family, who were nearly bursting at the seams, waiting for her to say yes so they could spend the rest of the evening celebrating the new couple. It was everything she'd thought she wanted.

It was just the wrong brother down on one knee.

Eleven

Sawyer could step aside because his father told him to. He could even take his brother shopping to pick out the ring he knew she would love. But he just couldn't sit at that table and watch Finn propose to the woman Sawyer loved.

Realizing that he loved Kat mere seconds before his brother stood up to make his big speech was Sawyer's typical poor timing. Before that, he'd known he cared about Kat and the baby. He liked spending time with her. If marrying her made her feel better about raising her daughter, he was willing to do it, and spare Finn from a fate he saw as worse than death. Sawyer knew he didn't like the idea of his brother with Kat. But until that moment, none of it had added up in his mind to love.

When he realized the truth, it was too much for him to take. He'd been in love before, so he should've realized it sooner. But he was stubborn. He knew Kat was never meant to be his, so he hadn't recognized the signs. How stupid could he be, to fall in love with the woman having his brother's child? Even after he knew she wanted to marry Finn for the child's sake, he couldn't stay away. The whole situation was doomed from their first kiss that day at the District.

So he left. Simple as that. His parents would probably be annoyed. He'd have to explain that he realized he'd forgotten an appointment or something. Left the iron on at home. He certainly couldn't tell them he was in love with Kat and didn't want to watch her get engaged to Finn.

His phone rang several times on his drive home that night, but he didn't answer. He put it on Silent and shoved it into the glove box of his Audi. He didn't want to hear about how it went. He didn't want to see a picture of the blissful couple. He just wanted to go home, drink a beer and reevaluate his damn life.

What he certainly didn't expect was to find his brother sitting in his office the next morning.

When he opened the door, Finn was reclining casually on the leather sofa he kept near the window for visits and late afternoon naps.

"Good morning, brother," Finn said in a chipper tone.

Too chipper, to tell the truth. Sawyer looked at him with mistrust, going past the couch to toss his laptop bag onto the desk. "It's too early for you to be up."

"I'm still on Beijing time. I figure since I'm just going back in a few weeks, I shouldn't bother fighting the time difference and the jet lag."

"I figured you were out all night celebrating your pending nuptials."

Finn's brow furrowed in confusion. "Nuptials? You mean you haven't heard?"

Sawyer sighed and leaned against his desk. "Haven't heard what, Finn? It's too early for guessing games."

"You haven't looked at your phone!" Finn got up from the couch and walked over to him. "Hold out your hand," he said.

When Sawyer complied, Finn dropped the ring box into his palm. He opened it, expecting it to be empty, with the ring on Kat's finger, but it was still safely nestled in its velvet bed. "Tell me you didn't chicken out on her!" he said, gripping the ring box in his fist and slamming the lid shut. He would punch Finn in the face right now if he'd changed his mind and broken Kat's heart.

"No way!" Finn said, as he ducked out of arm's reach. "I did my part. Pretty well, too. I didn't want to hear about it from Dad later, so I had a very nice, heartfelt proposal prepared. But she turned me down. Flat."

Sawyer froze for a moment. A part of him was waiting for Finn to say he was joking, but the relieved smile on his face said it all. Kat hadn't accepted his proposal and Finn was thrilled, because there was nothing their father could do about it.

"She said no?"

"She said *no*. With Dad and everyone else there to witness it. And while I'm relieved... I also have to say that I'm a bit concerned about why she changed her mind."

"Concerned?"

"Yes. Concerned that while I was out of the country, my twin brother may have swooped in and snatched Kat right out from under me."

"What are you talking about?"

"Come on, man. I saw you two looking at each other all evening. I asked you to handle the situation until I got back. I didn't mean sleep with her. What if I'd wanted to marry her? What if I'd really liked the idea of us starting our family together? You would've screwed it all up for everyone."

"Like that would've ever happened. You were only proposing because Dad was making you. And besides that, you never would've been in this situation if you hadn't gone to that party pretending to be me. She went there looking for me, not you. So don't try to act all innocent and put out. If anyone swooped in and stole anything, *you* tried to snatch Kat away from *me*."

"Yeah, well, now you have your shot. I'm off the hook with Dad and she's all yours."

Sawyer narrowed his gaze at his brother with contempt. "No matter what you do, you always seem to get away with it."

"What is that supposed to mean?"

"It means that I've never met someone so reckless, so irresponsible, and yet you never get what's coming to you. You never pay the price for your actions. Somehow you always get off the hook. You don't have to marry the mother of your child. You didn't have to pay when you wrecked Tom's motorcycle. Dad smoothed things over when you got in trouble in school. No matter what happens, you never have to clean up your messes. You always get one of us to handle everything for you, and then you have the audacity to get irritable with me because I happened to fall in love with the girl you're supposed to be with?"

Finn opened his mouth, but stopped short of

answering. His angry retort seemed to deflate inside him. He looked at his brother for a moment and shook his head. "Are you serious? You're in love with her?"

Sawyer clenched his jaw in irritation with himself for letting that slip. He and Finn didn't have the kind of relationship many twins had. They didn't share intimate details of their lives. Sawyer didn't want to hear about Finn's shenanigans and Finn was bored by most of what Sawyer did with his time. So this was a big moment for them both. An awkward one, too.

"Yes, I am," he said, turning away and putting the engagement ring box on the edge of his desk.

"And what the hell were you going to do if she accepted my proposal? Mope until the end of time?"

"I'm sure your marriage wouldn't have lasted that long," Sawyer quipped.

"Very funny," Finn said. "I'm being serious."

Sawyer shrugged. He hadn't really thought that far ahead. "Maybe moping. Maybe working myself into a bout of middle-aged hypertension. If she accepted your proposal, maybe I would've asked to take over in Beijing, and disappeared for a while. I thought she wanted to marry you. I wasn't going to interfere, no matter how I felt."

"Why not? You're always interfering in my life when you think I'm doing the wrong thing."

"*Because*…nothing was going to change the reality of the situation, and that was that Kat is having *your* child. Whether I loved her, whether she hated you. That's still *your* baby and I couldn't get in the way of that."

Finn dropped down into the guest chair and considered his brother's confession for a few minutes. "Does she love you?" he asked.

"I don't know." Sawyer followed suit and flopped down into his own desk chair with a heavy sigh. "We never really talked about it."

"But you said that she did want to marry me."

"I thought so. That's what she told Jade and Morgan on the Fourth of July."

"And yet, just a few short days later, she turned me down and made me look like an idiot in front of the whole family. I'd say she did some hard thinking since then. She's got to be in love with you. That's the only reason I could fathom."

"Because there's no way a woman wouldn't want to marry you otherwise?"

"I'm a catch, damn it. And so are you. I say she's in love with you."

Sawyer sat forward and rested his elbows on his knees. "Even if she is…what about your daughter?"

Finn paused and looked at his brother with surprise. His mouth dropped open as he scrambled for words. "She's... Kat's... *We're* having a girl?"

"Oh." Sawyer sat up straight, alarmed at letting that slip. "I didn't realize she hadn't told you yet. I'm sorry. The whole family knows. Morgan turned the yacht pink when we sailed on the Fourth."

Finn shook his head. "We didn't really get to chat about much, with everyone there. A daughter...wow. A daughter is exciting news. Perhaps a little bit of karma for me."

"Perhaps."

"And despite what you might think, I plan to be a part of my daughter's life. I might be a shameless flirt with commitment issues, but I'm not a deadbeat dad. Kat and I can work out the details, but I'll be involved with the baby. As for the mother..." His voice trailed off. "She obviously wants you. She should be with you."

Finn cupped the ring box on the edge of the desk and slid it across the smooth wood to Sawyer, who reached out and caught it before it could fall to the floor. "Take that," Finn said. "Give it to her. Hell, you're the one that picked it out, anyway. You knew what she would like. I'm sure she'd appreciate it a lot more coming from you."

"No, you should return it."

"Nah," Finn said. "There's no way I can walk

back in there with a ring that expensive and tell the man at the counter that the woman said no. You take it or I'll stash it in a drawer somewhere and forget about it until some girl staying over finds it hidden away and thinks I'm about to propose. No thanks."

"It was expensive."

"So was that Jet Ski," Finn admitted. "And since I made you give it to me to go to that party for you, like a jerk, why don't we call it an even trade?"

Sawyer couldn't believe his ears. He'd dropped nearly twenty grand on that Jet Ski and yet it didn't come close to the price of Kat's ring. But he realized this was Finn's way of saying he was sorry. His pride wouldn't let him voice the words, not even to Sawyer. But he meant it in his way.

Getting up from his chair, Sawyer walked around the desk and stood in front of his brother with the velvet box in his hand. "You're sure?"

"Take it. Give it to her. Live happily ever after with the mother of my child," Finn said, as he rose to his feet. "Yes, you'll be my daughter's stepdad/uncle and I'll be her dad/uncle, but who cares about labels? We'll all raise our daughter together in whatever weird way makes sense for us, and it's nobody's damn business but ours."

Sawyer looked at Finn with amazement, and for the first time in a long time, felt the urge to give him a hug. He actually couldn't remember the last time he'd hugged his brother. But before he could do so, Finn surprised him and reached out to him instead. He wrapped his arms around Sawyer and patted him firmly on the back.

"Be good to them," he said. Then he turned and walked out of Sawyer's office without another word.

Kat had a million things to do before the District shut down in a few days. She hadn't done a single thing in preparation for the baby. She needed to clean house and buy groceries. So naturally, she was sitting on her piazza drinking tea and reading a book. It was a bestselling self-help title she'd picked up from the library. The author promised to help her identify her own self-sabotaging habits and live her best life.

So far it was stupid. But it was easier to read than think about what kind of disaster her life had turned into lately.

Some people would say things weren't that bad. She'd chosen not to marry a man who was all wrong for her. She supposed that was for the best, even if she did have to turn down Finn in front of his family. Despite that hurdle, her relationship with Finn may have actually become better for the rejection. He'd obviously been pressured to make the proposal and seemed relieved when she turned him down.

They'd had lunch together a few days later and finally got the opportunity to talk without anyone else around. Without interfering fathers and over-protective attorneys, they'd hammered out a plan to co-raise their daughter that made them both happy. Finn agreed to pay for private schools, and would be buying a place closer to Kat, with a bedroom for nights he had custody. Kat hadn't really wanted or needed his money, but would accept the child support payments he insisted on, given that he reduce the monthly amount in favor of setting up a trust fund for the baby that she would get when she turned twenty-one.

It was all very civilized.

And if Kat had heard from Sawyer since he'd walked out of that family dinner, she might feel better about how it was all turning out. But she hadn't.

Perhaps she had read the whole situation wrong. Sawyer had told her he didn't have any reason why she shouldn't marry Finn. Maybe he'd been telling the truth. Maybe he wanted her only because he knew he couldn't have her. She was a forbidden temptation. And now she was just a single, pregnant lady. Not very tempting at all.

The sound of the doorbell caused Kat to sit up

and set the book aside. Glancing out, she noticed a black Rolls Royce parked on the street. She went to the door and opened it, finding none other than Ingrid Steele standing on her stoop.

"Mrs. Steele? I mean, Ingrid?" She corrected herself. "What are you doing here?"

"I'm paying a call on my future granddaughter-in-law," she said. "May I come in?"

Startled, Kat took a step back and welcomed the older woman inside. "Would you like to sit on the piazza or in the house? I'll get us both a glass of tea."

"The piazza and tea sound lovely."

Kat rushed into the house to get some tea and returned to find Ingrid sitting patiently on one of her patio chairs. She handed her the glass and wished she had some kind of cookies or treats in the house to offer. Unfortunately, all she'd bothered to get at the grocery store of late were saltine crackers, cereal and granola bars. She wasn't sure if it was morning sickness carrying into the second trimester or if she was just nauseated by how awful things had become. Either way, chopped-up chocolate chip granola bars on a platter wouldn't quite cut it for the Steele matriarch.

"I didn't expect to see you today," Kat began. "Or for a while, considering how dinner ended the other night."

"Pish posh. You're family now, dear. The other night doesn't change that."

All things considered, Kat appreciated the sentiment. The Steeles weren't the average American family, but they were the closest thing she had. "She will be your great-granddaughter, of course," Kat said, rubbing her belly. It seemed to be growing a bit more every morning of late. "But I'm just...me."

"Well, maybe I'm old and sentimental, but I still think you'll be my granddaughter-in-law someday."

"You know that Finn and I aren't going to marry, right? He never really wanted to marry me. I think he only proposed because Trevor put him up to it."

Ingrid chuckled and shook her head. "Of course Trevor made him do it. But I'm not talking about Finn, dear. I'm talking about you and Sawyer."

Kat looked up from her tea in surprise. As far as she was aware, no one knew about what had happened between her and Sawyer. She forced the mouthful of tea down her throat without choking and asked, "What would make you say that?"

"I may be old, but I'm not blind, dear. There's been something simmering between you two this whole time. I saw that much at my garden party and during the Fourth of July gathering. It didn't matter that you rarely spoke and never touched. You were always stealing glances at each other when the other wasn't looking. I could feel the sexual tension in the air. If you were trying to hide how you feel, you were doing a terrible job, both of you."

Kat didn't bother to argue with her. There was no sense in lying about it now that things with Finn were settled. "Well, I honestly don't know how Sawyer feels about me. He never said anything."

"That doesn't mean much. Men are always stubborn about their feelings, especially in this family. I shouldn't say so, but Sawyer is my favorite grandchild. Even as a baby he was more serious and thoughtful. He would quietly sit in the grass and study a butterfly, while his brother ran through the yard, terrorizing everything in his path. He is my quiet grandchild, but still waters run deep in him. Just because he doesn't say it doesn't mean he doesn't feel it. How did he treat you?"

"When we weren't arguing...like gold."

"That sounds about right. Did you ever tell him how you felt?"

She gave a guilty shake of her head. "No. I was afraid to. And I kept telling myself that I should be with Finn, even though I knew it felt wrong. I thought it was best for the baby."

"What's best for the baby is what will make

you happy, dear. Babies don't know anything about DNA or legitimacy. They just want to be surrounded by love and warmth. Don't you think Sawyer could give her that?"

"Absolutely. But he's not here. I haven't seen him since he ran out on dinner that night."

"I'm sure he's sitting at home wrestling with the situation, just like you are. He didn't bolt from the room in the middle of your brother's proposal because he had food poisoning. He couldn't bear to sit there and watch the woman he loved get engaged to someone else. I guarantee it."

"Yes, well, it's been days and I'm sure he's heard how it turned out by now. If he was trying to be a gentleman and let Finn have his chance first, it's done. He hasn't even texted to ask how I am."

Ingrid sipped her tea and then set it aside. "Sawyer is a lot like his grandfather in many ways. Maybe that's why I've always had such a soft spot in my heart for him. They're both perfectionists. Strategists. The two of them would play a single chess match for hours in the library. They didn't like to make a decision or move on a project until everything was just so. That might make them seem like they're slow to act, but once they've made a decision, they're absolutely certain they're making the right choice."

"So he's sitting at home trying to decide if he really wants me?"

"No, no. More than likely, he's plotting and planning how to woo you properly."

Kat wasn't sure she'd ever been wooed. But whatever he was planning—if anything—she wished he would go ahead and do it. She didn't like being in limbo.

"I wish I were as confident as you are," she said. "I asked him if he could tell me a reason why I shouldn't marry Finn, and he said he couldn't."

"Of course he couldn't. He wouldn't interfere if he thought that was what you wanted. It doesn't mean he didn't want to give you a reason. He probably could've named five reasons why you shouldn't marry Finn, without trying very hard. But he didn't believe it was the right thing to do."

"You think so?"

"I've seen my grandchildren grow from head-strong toddlers to corporate leaders and entrepreneurs. I know how they think. And I know," Ingrid said, as she reached out to cup Kat's cheek, "that he cares for you. Just give him time. I have faith that if you want to be a Steele, you will be before too long."

Ingrid looked down at her watch. "Well, dear, this was a lovely visit, but I've got to get going. I have an appointment to see my jeweler." She got up and slipped her purse over her arm.

Kat stood and followed her to the door. "Thank you for stopping by. I feel better about everything."

"I'm glad, dear. I'll be awaiting news."

Kat watched Ingrid go down her walkway and over to where a man was waiting to open the door to the Rolls. Once she'd settled inside, he shut the door and got in to drive her to her jeweler, or wherever her agenda was taking her next.

As the car disappeared around the next block, Kat let the piazza door close and returned to her spot on the sofa. She shoved the book to the other side of the cushions and thought over everything Ingrid had told her.

Perhaps Sawyer *was* sitting in his house, trying to decide on the perfect way to woo her. But she had no guarantees of that, just a confident grandmother. He could just as easily be working on his renovation plans for the District. That was right around the corner, and despite her best efforts, Kat was unable to stop it from happening. She was right back where she'd started, although now she had a baby on the way and a broken heart to complicate things.

That said, Kat wasn't the kind to sit around and wait on a man to decide what he wanted. She had a studio to relocate and a baby to plan for, so she would focus on what she could control. And if he ever showed up with his heart in his hands, maybe she wouldn't stomp on it the way he'd stomped on hers.

Twelve

It was the last day for the District as Kat knew it and loved it. By five today, everyone had to be gone, for renovations to begin. Most of the tenants had already moved out, leaving the old warehouse hollow and empty sounding, when it had once been filled with life and art.

She did love Sawyer, but a part of her would never forgive him for turning this place into some high-end mini-mall for people who liked to be seen as art savvy. Even if he just made repairs and re-opened, it wouldn't be the same. Most of the people she knew wouldn't be returning, because they couldn't afford the rent. With each artist who had packed up and gone forever, the District lost a little bit of its soul.

Kat wasn't sure what she was going to do. She was one of the few who could afford the new rent. She just wasn't certain she wanted to come back. It wouldn't be the same without Hilda and Zeke arguing, or the little chocolate shop owner coming around to test a new recipe on willing volunteers.

Kat's place had an old outbuilding at the head of the driveway that had once been the kitchen. It got so hot in Charleston during the summer that the early homes had been built with the kitchen separate from the rest. Kat's had been converted years later into a storage room when a new kitchen was added to the house, but it wouldn't take much to put her equipment out there. That would be more convenient, especially with the baby, but it wouldn't be the same.

As she opened the door to her studio, even it felt like its soul was gone. All her work and most of her tools were already packed up and gone. The movers had come the day before to take her bigger pieces of equipment and the giant owl that was too heavy for her to move. Today, she was taking a few last items off the walls and closing up shop.

The final thing, the most important thing, was for her to remove the sign above the shop door. The wooden plaque had been one of the first pieces she'd made when her father gifted her with some basic woodworking tools on her sixteenth birthday. The hand-carved sign had a crescent moon and stars etched around the edges, with a textured background that looked like cumulous clouds once she'd applied the dark oak stain and sealant. In the center were the words *Wooden Dreams*.

She had made the sign long before the idea of having her own studio developed. Her father had hung it proudly in the house, where it had stayed until after they'd passed and Kat sold her parents' home. After college, when she'd heard about spaces available at the District, she'd gone down to pick a location and knew exactly where the sign needed to be. It wasn't her best work, but it was one of her favorites, and Wooden Dreams became the name of her shop.

Looking up at it hanging there now, Kat felt the tears start to come.

Just one more item in the list of things she'd lost over the last few weeks. She'd lost her shop, her artist community, her chance at a family and, apparently, she'd lost her heart to a man too honorable to admit how he felt about her. Altogether, it was almost enough to send her back to the dark place she'd lived in after her parents died. Her little girl was the only thing keeping her going.

And a little bit of hope. Hope that Sawyer might change his mind.

At least, if Grandma Ingrid was right to begin with. If she was wrong, then Kat had just given away her heart to someone who had no desire to take it. Either way, she hadn't heard a peep from Sawyer. Finn had called to let her know he was heading back to China, and Jade had texted her about setting up a date for a baby shower, but other than that, it was like before the baby, when there were no Steeles in her life.

She had to admit life was simpler then. And lonelier. But she loved her daughter's new family. So at least she had that.

In the empty cavern of the warehouse, the grind of the freight elevator was audible even on the far side where Kat's studio was located. She didn't pay much attention to it, though. It was probably another tenant here to load up their dreams and memories into cardboard boxes.

Instead, Kat unfolded her stepladder to take down her sign. On the second step, she couldn't quite grasp it, so she climbed to the third, which she hated because she felt so unsteady. Thankfully, she was able to hold on to the door frame as she reached up with her other hand to get the sign.

"Whoa," she said aloud, when the unexpected weight of the freed wooden panel threw off her balance. Her center of gravity was all out of whack because of the baby.

"Easy now," someone said, and she felt strong hands at her lower back and hip steadying her.

Kat tucked the sign under her arm and looked around to see who was there. To her surprise, it was Sawyer.

"Hand it to me," he said. "It will make it easier for you to get down."

She reluctantly passed him the sign and climbed down to the wood plank floors. Once she was on firm ground again, she snatched the sign from Sawyer and turned her back on him to return to her shop. While a part of her was happy to see him after all this time, he was the reason she was packing up today, hovering on the verge of tears.

"Kat?" Sawyer called after her in confusion.

"I appreciate your help in keeping me from falling, but why are you here?" she asked. "I haven't heard from you since the dinner party for your brother and then you show up out of the blue. It can't be just to see me or you wouldn't have waited so long. It must be because of the building. Are you here to make sure I don't chain myself to the front doors or something?"

Sawyer appeared contrite. He tucked his hands into his pants pockets and looked down at the ground the way he always did when he was thinking. "I'm sorry, Kat."

She put the sign into the last box she had left in the studio, and then turned around to face him. "Sorry about what? About closing this place down and uprooting everyone and everything I care about? About refusing to tell me how you felt for me, at the critical moment when I had to decide if I wanted to marry your brother? About disappearing off the face of the earth after I turned Finn down, making me wonder if I was crazy or just plain stupid for falling for you?"

He stood there and took every angry word she had to level at him. And when she was done, he reached into his breast coat pocket and pulled out an envelope addressed to her. "I'm sorry for all of it," he said.

Sawyer held out the envelope until Kat reluctantly took it from him. In the corner the address was imprinted for the District Arts Center. But it wasn't her District. This was his, with a fancy new logo to go with the new vision. She tore through the logo as she opened the envelope and pulled out the single-page notice inside.

Her eyes quickly scanned what was written, but she kept having to stop and go back because it didn't make any sense. She couldn't be reading the words she was reading. Starting back at the top, she went through it word by word, hoping this time she could believe what she saw.

It was an official letter from Sawyer's development company about the closure today. It stated that they expected to complete the necessary renovations in three months. At that time, any previous tenants who wanted to return to their studio would be grandfathered in to rent it at their current rate. Any new tenants would pay the higher rates.

Kat's hand began to tremble as she reached the end of the letter, making it hard to read. Especially while her eyes were overflowing with tears. Sawyer was going to fix the place up so it was safe, and let them return. Hilda and Zeke could reopen their studios. They could all do so if they chose to.

It was an incredible compromise and it made her angry that she hadn't thought of that first. But of course, Sawyer the Strategist had.

"Oh no," Sawyer said, whipping a pressed handkerchief from his pocket. "You're crying. I'm sorry. Please don't cry, Kat. I thought you would be happy."

She accepted the hankie, pressing it to her eyes and dabbing the tears from her cheeks. "I am happy. It's just, I don't know, pregnancy hormones combined with everything else. Ignore the tears."

Sawyer reached out to wipe a fresh one from

her cheek with his thumb. "That's hard for me to do. I don't like seeing you cry."

Kat shook her head. "I can't help it. What changed your mind about all this?"

"Once I realized how I felt about you, and that I wanted to be with you, I knew something had to be done about the situation here. You are more important to me than the bottom line. It may take a while to make back my investment in the renovations, but it isn't a rush. I think what I have planned will allow the community here to continue safely, but also bring in more foot traffic. It's a win-win, as long as you're happy." Sawyer reached out to take her hand.

"I'm happy," she said, as he squeezed it gently. "Thank you. On behalf of everyone here, thank you."

"I was just thinking, what would be the greatest gift I could give Kat for an engagement present?"

She froze in place, her hand still in his. She was almost uncertain she'd heard what he'd said, since he continued talking as though he hadn't dropped a bomb in the conversation.

"A ring is traditional, of course, and I have one of those, too, but I really wanted to give you something that would have meaning for you. This place is what brought us together, in a way, so it seemed sort of poetic that it would be what would bring us back together…for as long as we both shall live. I love you, Kat. More than anything."

"You love me?" Kat asked, the letter slipping from her fingers to the ground.

"I do. And I hope that you feel the same way. I wasn't sure, so I'm taking a gamble here." Sawyer reached into the same pocket, this time pulling out a small velvet box. "Finn gave me the ring he proposed with. I knew you would like it, but it felt wrong to give you the same ring. I was going to buy a different one and then an opportunity came along that I couldn't pass up."

He opened the lid on the box, which looked a great deal older than the one Finn had presented to her. This ring was vintage, she presumed, without even looking at it. Once the box was fully open, Kat gasped at the sight.

The diamond ring was unlike anything she'd seen in the jewelry cases at the mall. It actually looked like a daisy. In the center was a large, round, canary-yellow diamond, surrounded by six smaller diamonds that were at least a third of a karat each. The flower was set in platinum, with leaves and vines engraved into the band. It was unique. Beautiful. And yet oddly familiar.

"This was the ring that my grandfather Edward gave Grandma Ingrid when he proposed. She wore it every day after that, even after he passed away, until a few days ago, when she gave it to me."

That's where she had seen it before. Ingrid had worn it every time she'd seen her. Except the last time, when she'd come by her house. Kat thought back to Ingrid's visit and her next stop, at the jeweler. Perhaps she'd been making plans then, having it cleaned or resized for Sawyer to give her.

"My grandparents were together for nearly sixty years. I don't know how many I have to offer you, but I will happily give you any that I have left. If you'll have me."

"Will you marry me, Katherine?"

Sawyer dropped to one knee as he said the words and then held his breath. He wasn't certain what the answer was going to be. He'd thought for sure she would accept Finn's proposal, but she didn't. She hadn't said that she loved him, either. She'd just gotten weepy when he said the words, making him nervously talk far more than he'd intended to. But now he'd asked the question, and all he could do was await the answer.

After an extended moment of silence, he was getting more and more nervous.

"Kat?" he asked.

She was looking down at him with tears in her eyes and her hand covering her mouth.

"Are you okay?"

She nodded before wiping at her tears and taking a deep breath. "Sawyer, are you sure you want to marry me?"

He flinched at the question. "I'm absolutely sure. At the moment, I'm concerned about you, though. It doesn't sound like you want to marry me."

"I do," she said quickly, then crouched down until her eyes were level with his. "But what about the baby?"

Sawyer frowned. "What about her?"

Kat swallowed hard and bit her bottom lip. "Are you going to be okay with raising another man's child? Your brother's child at that. It's not the ideal way to start out a relationship, much less a marriage."

"You're pregnant?" Sawyer asked, with mock dismay and surprise.

Kat punched him in the shoulder. "I'm serious. It's a lot to ask of you, to help me raise Finn's baby. You and I both know how he can be. I have no idea how involved he's really going to be in her life. I'm not going to pretend it isn't a big deal."

Sawyer understood her concerns. He'd spent the last week thinking all this through. He made sure every eventuality was thought through, every *t* crossed and every *i* dotted. He no longer had any doubts about what he wanted to do, so he had to make sure the next words he spoke were enough to convince her that it wasn't the issue she believed it to be.

"Kat, I love you. And I love that baby. I have since the first moment I saw her on the screen and heard her heartbeat echo through the examination room. Yes, she's my brother's child. But that's as close as she could possibly be without being my own. As far as I'm concerned, she's as much mine as she is Finn's daughter, and that's how I'm going to treat her.

"I want to be there for every doctor's appointment. I'm going to be there when she's born and I'll fight Finn to hold her first. I want to be there when she takes her first steps and says her first words. That baby is a part of you, and a part of Finn. And as much as he makes me crazy sometimes, you two are the most important people in my life. So that means this baby is going to be an amazing combination of the two of you. She's already the love of my life. The apple of my eye. And I'll love her just as much as I'll love any children that you and I may have together someday."

"Stop now, or I'm going to get jealous," Kat said through her tears.

Sawyer smiled and reached out to caress her cheek. "There's nothing to be jealous about. There's not going to be another woman in South Carolina who is as loved and adored as my wife will be. But first, she's got to accept my proposal." He slipped the ring out of the box and held it up to Kat. "So what do you say? Do you want to marry me and become Mrs. Sawyer Steele?"

Kat looked at him and nodded through her tears. "I do. Yes!" She held out her hand and let him slip the family heirloom onto her finger. "It fits perfectly," she said, before leaning in and giving Sawyer a kiss.

"I know this isn't how you wanted things to turn out, or the family you envisioned when you came looking for Finn that day—" Sawyer began.

"It's not," Kat interrupted. "It's so much better." She kissed him again and he knew that she was right.

Their future together would be perfectly imperfect.

Epilogue

"And with the cutting of this ribbon, I'm happy to declare that the District Art Center is now officially reopened!"

Sawyer gave the nod to Kat and she, along with several of her fellow artisans, used the ridiculously large scissors to cut the ribbon. The audience cheered and the media happily filmed the crowds as they pushed through the front door to see the new and improved District.

Kat was bursting with pride as Sawyer sidled up beside her and wrapped his arm around her ever expanding waist. She was just a week into her third trimester now and she was starting to feel like an overfilled balloon. She couldn't imagine getting bigger and yet she had nearly three months left to go. Beatrice Astrid Steele, or Sweet Bea, as Sawyer referred to her, would be arriving sometime around Christmas. It was the best present she could ever expect.

The renovation of the District was a close second. Sawyer and his team had done amazing work on the building. It was basically a gut job, by necessity, but now there were sound floors covered in ceramic tile, ceilings that weren't on the verge of falling onto anyone's head, electrical and plumbing systems that worked and a new, blessed addition—air-conditioning and insulation. The open space around the warehouse was redone, too, with benches and fountains, trees, and an outdoor amphitheater for musical and theatrical performances. Later tonight, one of the local bands was going to be playing a concert to celebrate the reopening.

Kat and Sawyer followed the crowd inside. Most of the former artisans had returned, but in the unrented studios and newly developed spaces, there were some additions. Not only did they gain new painters, jewelry makers and other crafters, but they got some food vendors, too. A Mediterranean falafel place opened up near the entrance, an artisan Popsicle shop was on the third floor and a cupcake bakery—Kat's favorite stop—was on the ground floor.

There were no commercial chains, something Sawyer had promised her, but there was definitely a nice, upscale feel about the place now. Yes, there were artists at work, but it didn't feel like they were squatters in an abandoned warehouse any longer. It felt like they belonged, and their art was something worth coming to the District to see and, hopefully, to buy.

As they reached Kat's studio, with her Wooden Dreams sign in place, she was surprised to see there were already a few people eyeing her work. She kissed Sawyer on the cheek and went over to chat with her potential new customers.

A few minutes and a sale later, she turned back to find Sawyer on the phone. His face was as white as it had been the day he'd found out she was pregnant with Finn's child. Something was wrong.

She waited on eggshells until he ended the call and then turned to her. "What is it?" she asked.

"There's been an accident. Finn's private jet back from Beijing lost radio contact somewhere near the West Coast. They think the plane went down near Portland, Oregon."

Kat brought her hand to her mouth in shock. "Oh my God. Do they know if anyone survived?"

Sawyer shook his head. "They don't know. Rescue crews are searching for the plane in the woods and out at sea, but without a good idea of where it might've gone down, it might be a while before we know for sure if Finn is dead or alive."

* * * * *

Find out what happens to Finn in the next book in Andrea Laurence's Switched! miniseries.

WE HOPE YOU
ENJOYED THIS BOOK!

Experience sensual stories of juicy drama and intense chemistry cast in the world of the American elite.

Discover six new books every month, available wherever books are sold!

Harlequin.com

AVAILABLE THIS MONTH FROM
Harlequin® Desire

FROM BOARDROOM TO BEDROOM
Texas Cattleman's Club: Inheritance • by Jules Bennett

Sophie Blackwood needs the truth to take back what rightfully belongs to her family. Working for media CEO Nigel Townshend is the way to do it. What she doesn't expect is their undeniable attraction. Will her feelings for her British playboy boss derail everything?

BLAME IT ON THE BILLIONAIRE
Blackout Billionaires • by Naima Simone

Nadia Jordan certainly didn't plan on spending the night with Grayson Chandler during the blackout, but the bigger surprise comes when he introduces her as his fake fiancée to avoid his family's matchmaking! But even a fake relationship can't hide their real chemistry...

RULE BREAKER
Dynasties: Mesa Falls • by Joanne Rock

Despite his bad-boy persona, Mesa Falls ranch owner Weston Rivera takes his job very seriously—a point he makes clear to meddlesome financial investigator April Stephens. Stranded together by a storm, their attraction is searing, but can it withstand their differences once the snow clears?

ONE LITTLE INDISCRETION
Murphy International • by Joss Wood

After their night of passion, auction house CEO Carrick Murphy and art detective Sadie Slade aren't looking for anything more. But when she learns she's pregnant, they must overcome their troubled pasts for a chance at lasting happiness...

HIS FORBIDDEN KISS
Kiss and Tell • by Jessica Lemmon

Heiress Taylor Thompson never imagined her night would end with kissing a mysterious stranger—let alone her reluctant date's older brother, Royce Knox! Their spark can't be denied, but will family and professional pressure keep them to just one kiss?

TEMPORARY WIFE TEMPTATION
The Heirs of Hansol • by Jayci Lee

To keep his role as CEO, Garrett Song needs to find a bride, and fast. And Natalie Sobol is the perfect candidate. But their marriage of convenience is rocked when real passion takes over. Can a bargain that was only supposed to be temporary last forever?

HDATMBPA0120

COMING NEXT MONTH FROM

DESIRE

Available February 4, 2020

#2713 FROM BOARDROOM TO BEDROOM
Texas Cattleman's Club: Inheritance • by Jules Bennett
Sophie Blackwood needs the truth to take back what rightfully belongs to her family. Working for media CEO Nigel Townshend is the way to do it. What she doesn't expect is their undeniable attraction. Will her feelings for her British playboy boss derail everything?

#2714 BLAME IT ON THE BILLIONAIRE
Blackout Billionaires • by Naima Simone
Nadia Jordan certainly didn't plan on spending the night with Grayson Chandler during the blackout, but the bigger surprise comes when he introduces her as his fake fiancée to avoid his family's matchmaking! But even a fake relationship can't hide their real chemistry...

#2715 RULE BREAKER
Dynasties: Mesa Falls • by Joanne Rock
Despite his bad-boy persona, Mesa Falls ranch owner Weston Rivera takes his job very seriously—a point he makes clear to meddlesome financial investigator April Stephens. Stranded together by a storm, their attraction is searing, but can it withstand their differences once the snow clears?

#2716 ONE LITTLE INDISCRETION
Murphy International • by Joss Wood
After their night of passion, auction house CEO Carrick Murphy and art detective Sadie Slade aren't looking for anything more. But when she learns she's pregnant, they must overcome their troubled pasts for a chance at lasting happiness...

#2717 HIS FORBIDDEN KISS
Kiss and Tell • by Jessica Lemmon
Heiress Taylor Thompson never imagined her night would end with kissing a mysterious stranger—let alone her reluctant date's older brother, Royce Knox! Their spark can't be denied, but will family and professional pressure keep them to just one kiss?

#2718 TEMPORARY WIFE TEMPTATION
The Heirs of Hansol • by Jayci Lee
To keep his role as CEO, Garrett Song needs to find a bride, and fast. And Natalie Sobol is the perfect candidate. But their marriage of convenience is rocked when real passion takes over. Can a bargain that was only supposed to be temporary last forever?

———

**YOU CAN FIND MORE INFORMATION ON UPCOMING HARLEQUIN TITLES,
FREE EXCERPTS AND MORE AT HARLEQUIN.COM.**

HDCNM0120

Get 4 FREE REWARDS!

We'll send you 2 FREE Books plus __2 FREE Mystery Gifts.__

Harlequin® Desire books feature heroes who have it all: wealth, status, incredible good looks... everything but the right woman.

FREE
Value Over
$20

YES! Please send me 2 FREE Harlequin® Desire novels and my 2 FREE gifts (gifts are worth about $10 retail). After receiving them, if I don't wish to receive any more books, I can return the shipping statement marked "cancel." If I don't cancel, I will receive 6 brand-new novels every month and be billed just $4.55 per book in the U.S. or $5.24 per book in Canada. That's a savings of at least 13% off the cover price! It's quite a bargain! Shipping and handling is just 50¢ per book in the U.S. and $1.25 per book in Canada.* I understand that accepting the 2 free books and gifts places me under no obligation to buy anything. I can always return a shipment and cancel at any time. The free books and gifts are mine to keep no matter what I decide.

225/326 HDN GNND

Name (please print)

Address   Apt. #

City   State/Province   Zip/Postal Code

Mail to the **Reader Service:**
IN U.S.A.: P.O. Box 1341, Buffalo, NY 14240-8531
IN CANADA: P.O. Box 603, Fort Erie, Ontario L2A 5X3

Want to try 2 free books from another series? Call 1-800-873-8635 or visit www.ReaderService.com.

HD20

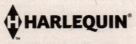